Come With Me

THE UNSOLVED KIDNAPPING THAT SHOCKED AND RIVETED TURN-OF-THE-CENTURY BUFFALO

Patrick Sawers

NFB Publishing
Buffalo, New York

NFB
NFB Publishing/Amelia Press
119 Dorchester Road
Buffalo, New York 14213

For Josie

Also by Patrick Sawers

The Way I Went Last Friday

Prologue

Trespassing fishermen had been making their way into the cemetery after hours, trampling all over the shrubbery and generally fouling up the meticulously-arranged landscaping.

As part of his nightly closeup routine, then, the superintendent had taken to dispatching a pair of workers over to that spot to check for invading anglers, and to shoo them off if necessary. One of these was his 23-year-old son, Robert Troup, who lived a few blocks away and was employed there as a florist. The other was a young man roughly the same age, an employee named George McGill.

It was a calm, still Friday night in June, and the gates of Forest Lawn Cemetery had been closed for over an hour.

Troup and McGill set out on their assignment sometime around 7:30 p.m., leaving the superintendent's quarters and roughly following along the path of a thin, meandering creek that came passing through the grounds, bisecting the graveyard's two hundred acres before opening up into a huge, manmade reservoir just beyond its western border. Right outside its gate the creek passed beneath a stone arch bridge, and regularly folks gathered on that overpass to drop a fishing line down into the gently-babbling stream below.

It was unusually quiet when the two men reached the bridge about fifteen minutes later, finding no fishermen in sight and the area seemingly free of undesirables. It was just the third day of summer, so the sun had yet to descend over the horizon and a fair amount of daylight remained. The pair decided to relax a while, kicking back and looking on as vehicles and bicyclists made their way across the bridge just outside the cemetery's six-foot high, picket-style wrought iron fence.

Just inside that gate was a separate, much smaller body of water, another artificial widening of the creek carried out a quarter-century earlier and named Swan Lake by its developers. Its northernmost tip formed a small cove, perhaps fifty feet long and thirty feet at its widest, and not at all very deep. It was a little before 8:30 p.m. when Troup and McGill decided to head back, but as they strolled along this cove Troup abruptly seized his partner's arm and drew him to a sharp halt.

"There's something in the water!" he exclaimed, pointing excitedly at a bundle of some sort sticking up out of the water's surface near the center of the cove, thirty or forty feet from its northern bank. After pausing to study the apparition for a moment, Troup added, "It looks like a head."

"Isn't that an arm sticking up there in the water?" volleyed McGill, equally stunned at the gruesome and distressing prospect.

"I think that it is the body of a little child," Troup concluded, "and we ought to get it out."

In order to draw the thing ashore – whatever it was – Troup went jogging over to a nearby supply shed to retrieve a plumb line, essentially a long pole with a weighted line attached to one end, generally used to determine the depth of water. McGill hung behind in order to keep watch over the unidentified floating object, and eventually Troup came running back with a long chalk line to which he'd tied a heavy lead sinker.

Right away he handed the thing over to McGill, who cast the weight well out into the water and watched as it landed a bit beyond his target. Slowly reeling the line back in, he managed to snag the parcel up and began drawing it a bit closer. It wasn't easy, and the thing came loose of the line a few times, but after three tense and trying minutes McGill was able to successfully wrangle it ashore.

The bundle lay there, half on land and half remaining in the muddy, stagnant waters of the tiny lake, and as the two moved in to inspect it they swiftly arrived at the same awful conclusion. Troup had been right. It was, in fact, the body of a little child.

A badly-decomposed head, one arm and a pair of tiny feet were all that was visible. The rest had been wrapped up in cloth and newspaper and then tied tightly at the ankles, waist and shoulders with what appeared to be several lengths of clothesline. It was a filthy, disgusting mess, encasing the badly-bloated remains of a poor, innocent child who had met the ghastliest fate imaginable, her unspeakable demise then concealed from the world in just several feet of rancid, bacteria-infested cemetery water.

After a solemn moment, it was McGill who broke the silence.

"I'll bet it is the missing Murphy girl."

Troup pondered this a moment, then declared that they'd best go ahead and report their sad discovery.

"I guess I'll go and tell father."

The Murphy girl had been missing for ten days, and her disappearance was the "reigning sensation" of the city, as one local newspaper put it. Last seen just steps from her own home, the child had been out playing and roaming the streets before bedtime, something the neighborhood kids did pretty much every night after excusing themselves from the dinner table. She'd never returned, though, and much of her parents' agony and growing anxiety was being echoed by the community at large. A full week and a half had passed with no sign of the girl, and a blanket of fear and paranoia now enveloped their quiet residential neighborhood not far from downtown.

Five-year-old Marian A. Murphy had vanished into thin air, or so it seemed to police investigators, who had been diligent in their search but gotten nowhere in terms of pinning down the little girl's whereabouts. Neighbors had been questioned, houses searched and canals and waterways dredged for any trace of the missing girl or her remains, but all to no avail. And despite a barrage of press coverage – the case certainly had the rapt attention of the city's curious and concerned citizenry – nothing true or significant had been uncovered and the popular belief, by this point, was that the child had either drowned or been carried off by transients or hobos.

But now, with the discovery of a small child's remains in an obscure cemetery pond three miles north of the missing girl's home, the search for Marian Murphy was about to come to a screeching halt. The question of her whereabouts had seemingly been answered, and in its place a host of new ones arose. Chief among these, naturally, was the matter of who had been responsible for the girl's disappearance and death, and the ensuing hunt for the guilty party would be massive and all-encompassing.

It was, the area papers all boldly decried, shaping up to be the most scandalous and salacious murder mystery in the city's brief history.

ONE

A West Side Story

A gray cloud was hanging over the city of Buffalo, New York, in the summer of 1902.

The city's history had been a rough and tumble one, but in the one hundred years since its founding it had charted an impressive and remarkable ascent. The 1825 opening of the Erie Canal, which reached its terminus at Buffalo thanks to the city's auspicious location right on Lake Erie, had caused its population to explode as industry took hold and businesses started thriving. By the middle of the nineteenth century Buffalo had become the grain-storage capital of the world, and its bustling manufacturing industry was a beacon for the immigrant laborers who would, over the years, lay the city's infrastructure and build it up into its present form.

By the dawn of the twentieth century Buffalo had grown to become the eighth-largest city in the country, with a population of around 350,000 and more millionaires per capita than any other city in the world. Business was booming all around, and city leaders had chosen to ring in the new century by showcasing the city's achievements on a global stage, hosting a World's Fair designed to draw in visitors and spectators from every corner of the country and even clear across the globe.

The 1901 Pan-American Exposition had done exactly that, taking place on 350 acres of undeveloped farmland north of the city, opening in May of that year and featuring displays and exhibits from a deluge of cultures across various countries. The exposition's major theme had been progress, and accordingly the occasion was used to introduce the world to alternating current, generated at nearby Niagara Falls and harnessed into 160,000 incandescent bulbs that illuminated the grounds nightly. There were tents and sideshows set up all around, featuring all manner of attractions from wild and exotic animals to in-person appearances by some of the country's most notorious daredevils.

What was to be the fair's zenith, however, had instead turned out to be its utter devastation, a citywide disgrace and the nation's first great trauma of the 1900s. On September 6, while greeting constituents at the exposition's Temple of Music, 25th United States President William McKinley was shot twice in the abdomen by a lone gunman named Leon Czolgosz, a 28-year-old Polish-American proletariat and anarchist extremist. Initial expectations were that the president would survive as he coalesced at the Delaware Avenue mansion of Pan-Am president John Milburn, but a week into his recovery things took a turn for the worse and McKinley passed away on September 14, casting a dense pall over the remainder of the expo and sullying the city's image for decades to come.

The Pan-Am had continued through November, although McKinley's assassination had shattered much of the jubilation and dampened most of the glory, and all told the exposition failed to meet its lofty financial expectations. It had been a whirlwind extravaganza, attended over its six-month course by more than eight million people, but by March 1902 work had begun on the slow, sad process of demolition. Much of the grand optimism and the excitement that had enveloped the city at the turn of the century had abated by that point, and the conviction and subsequent execution of the presidential assassin Czolgosz had done predictably little to restore levity.

But things weren't all bad, going into the summer of 1902. The standard of living, in fact, had never been higher. There was electricity in the homes and on the streets, and many residences were equipped with a telephone, making immediate communication the calling card of the new century. Automobiles did exist, but they were considered showy and newfangled and only the city's most fabulous were seen tooling around in them. Despite this the streets were freshly paved with asphalt, as Buffalo had been the first major American city to undertake that progressive endeavor.

* * * * * *

A little over three miles to the south of the expo's ruins, on Buffalo's lower west side, a patch of side-by-side residential properties make up the Lakeview neighborhood, so-named because its western perimeter touches right up against the shore of Lake Erie, a bit north of all the silos and the grain elevators down by the bustling harbor.

Roughly a quarter of a square mile in size, the neighborhood was quiet, residential and walking distance from downtown, featuring nice-sized homes with ample backyards and a plethora of nearby churches, schools and parks. Just beyond its northeastern border lie the adjacent Allentown neighborhood, a former tract of farmland that was then becoming a magnet for eager young go-getters looking to shed their rural roots in favor of a more urban and exciting living experience.

The area's most defining property, up until the previous year anyhow, had been the one-time home of former Buffalo mayor William G. Fargo, who had built his fortune as the co-founder of both American Express and, later, Wells Fargo & Company. Upon his retirement Fargo had commissioned a 22,000-square-foot French Mansard-style estate – the largest and most extravagant in the entire city – to be constructed in the dead center of a five-and-a-half-acre city block bordered by Fargo Avenue, Jersey Street, West Avenue and Pennsylvania Street.

The home, completed in 1871, had hosted a variety of prominent guests and dignitaries, ranging from the writer Mark Twain to former United States presidents Grover Cleveland and Ulysses S. Grant, but with Fargo's passing in 1881 the elaborately-scaped property began to stagnate and fall into disrepair. For the past decade the home had stood there vacant and abandoned, and finally the previous year it had met its demolition. What remained was an entire city block in ruins, a heavily-treed field dotted with heaps of rubble and debris, and the spot had become a compelling one for neighborhood kids out exploring their environs.

A good number of Irish also seemed to inhabit the Lakeview neighborhood at that time, at least judging by the names listed in the Buffalo City Directory of 1902. Residents were, as one local newspaper put it, "variously classed as to wealth," and it was a neighborhood where "some are rich, others moderately well off and others with nothing more than a living."

The occupants of the small, two-story house at 257 West Avenue fell into that latter category, for the most part. The home stood kitty-corner to the Fargo property, just across Pennsylvania and on the other side of West, one house removed from the eastern corner of that intersection. It has since been demolished – a plot of densely-woven arborvitae occupies the spot today – but at the time the place was home to Cornelius and Mary Murphy, a middle-aged couple with four young children.

As a turn-of-the-century middle-class Irish Catholic, 37-year-old Cornelius V. Murphy wasn't particularly successful, although he was a long way from having to labor on the docks of the nearby First Ward, like so many who had occupied his station just a generation earlier. Born in December 1864 to Irish immigrant parents, he was employed as a subscription agent in the office of the *Catholic Union and Times*, a local weekly publication servicing Buffalo's growing Catholic population. He was, by all accounts, a man of limited means – "far from affluent," as one local paper would later put it, while another regarded him as "not particularly well to do."

Still, Cornelius did enjoy a reputation for being a diligent and extremely hard worker, always willing to stay late, travel for business or go the extra mile in general. And while this won him the respect and admiration of his colleagues, it did not go unnoticed that he seemed extremely prone to overexertion, and that he tended to work himself to the very brink. His demeanor was gruff, rigid and often abrasive, while his manner of speaking was sharp, curt and occasionally quite loud. This all went hand-in-hand with his blunt and stocky build; he was described by one paper as "a thick, heavy set man, rather short in stature," with a "thick and heavy" neck and hair that was "dark and closely cropped in the back."

In 1893 Cornelius had taken a bride, a young lady five years his junior – "a thin, dark-complexioned woman, not very tall" – named Mary E. O'Brien. Born in New Jersey to Irish immigrant parents, Mary had been orphaned at a young age and subsequently taken in by an aunt who lived with her own children in Jersey City. Her aunt's family was of considerable means, it seems, and Mary had in fact been the initial mortgage holder on the couple's small West Avenue home.

The Murphys had welcomed their first child in June of 1894, a baby girl they'd named Angela, although she would grow up often using her middle name, Jane, throughout much of her childhood. Their next came just over two years later, on July 18, 1896, another girl they'd named Marian, although frequently she was referred to simply as Mary, like her mother. On June 30, 1898, a third child was born, a son to bear his father's name; young Cornelius, though, generally was called by his middle name, Leo.

The family had, by that point, weathered some considerable internal turmoil, much of it owing to the increasingly-erratic behavior of its brash and short-tempered patriarch. This all began with the death of his wife's foster mother, the wealthy aunt who had taken her in and raised her back in Jersey City. In her will the woman had left a considerable sum to each of her biological children, however Mary, technically her niece, received a much smaller amount. This had incensed Cornelius, who formally contested the will but had ultimately been defeated in court. "That," one newspaper noted, "is said to have unsettled his mind."

Another local paper, back in June 1899, had covered his bizarre meltdown:

The troubles of Cornelius V. Murphy, 289 Pennsylvania street, began a few days ago, when he swore out a warrant for the arrest of his brother, Michael, charging with theft of a deed. After his brother had been locked up Murphy found the deed. He withdrew the warrant and Michael was released.

On complaint of Frank Zirheld, a butcher, Murphy was arrested Wednesday on a charge of passing a worthless check for $20. He was afterwards bailed out. Yesterday he was arraigned before Justice Graf. An arrangement was made whereby Murphy was released after depositing with the Justice three gold watches as security for the payment of the check.

Early yesterday afternoon Murphy, while riding his wheel down Franklin street, collided with Mrs. William Stokes, 379 Niagara street. Both were thrown to the pavement and slightly bruised. A policeman took a statement from Murphy and let him go.

Not long after that Murphy was crossing Swan street at the corner of Franklin street, when he was recognized by Seth Huson, a jeweler at 332 Connecticut street. Huson claims Murphy purchased three watches from him, paying for them with a check for $87, which the jeweler, it is said, afterwards found worthless. The watches were the ones that Murphy had left with Justice Graf.

Huson went to the Franklin Street Station and requested that an officer be sent with him to arrest the man. Detective Dugan was detailed and found Murphy standing in front of the office of the Catholic Union and Times. Dugan asked Murphy to walk to the station house with him, but Murphy refused to do so. He put up such a fight that reinforcements had to be summoned. Huson preferred a charge of grand larceny against the prisoner.

It is claimed by the police that Murphy passed a check for $10 on Matthew Ring, commission merchant at 246 Front avenue, and one for $7 on P.F. Sands, a letter carrier living at 8 York street.

Murphy was once an inmate of the Buffalo State Hospital. Physicians will examine him as to his mental condition.

He'd then been carted off to the jailhouse, and according to yet another publication his behavior there was similarly unhinged: "He had not been there long when he began to act queerly," that newspaper wrote. "He seemed to think he was in a hotel and that Jailer Brennan was the proprietor. He commanded an attendant, whom he thought was a bellboy, to bring him some ice water. When it was brought he grumbled that it was too warm. He kept this up day after day and otherwise made trouble for the attendants. Several times he set fire to the bedclothing to his cell and the last time narrowly escaped setting himself on fire. Finally, a few days ago, the jailer called in some brain experts and had him examined. The result was he was sent to the State Hospital."

Looking back on those events, another paper carried a different, rather time-distorted version: "The police have been told that two years ago Murphy was very violent. Just prior to that time he had gained great notoriety by ordering a vast quantity of goods sent to his house, C.O.D., and the street at time was crowded with delivery wagons, containing goods sent in this manner. The goods were all returned to the various merchants and in the end Murphy was sent to the State Hospital. At that time he conceived the delusion that Mrs. Murphy was conspiring against him and Mrs. Murphy's presence in the same room was sufficient to give him violent paroxysms of rage and fury. Mrs. Murphy is said to have been afraid of her life at that time."

All told, it's said that Cornelius spent about three years in remand at the local psychiatric facility, spread out over three separate occasions. The Buffalo State Asylum for the Insane, more commonly referred to as Buffalo State Hospital, was located north of the city on two hundred acres at the northwestern intersection of Forest and Elmwood Avenues, just a few blocks south of the future Pan-Am site. Opened in 1880, the complex had been designed by the architect Henry Hobson Richardson, with lush, rolling grounds beautifully laid out by Frederick Law Olmsted so as to encourage a restful and relaxing period of recuperation (the facility was shuttered in the mid-1970s, although it has since been rehabbed and restored, added to the National Register of Historic Places and opened to the public as the Richardson Hotel).

Upon his third and final discharge from that facility doctors pronounced Cornelius "cured," however they also cautioned that he did run the risk of becoming "permanently insane" later in life. This sort of thing, one of his relatives quietly confessed, ran in Cornelius's family.

Just several weeks earlier, in late May of 1902, Cornelius and Mary had welcomed their fourth child, another boy to balance out their brood. And while the baby John was no doubt a delight to his older siblings especially, his mother for several months had been suffering from what doctors were calling "nervous prostration" – essentially a breakdown due to exhaustion – and the stress of an added infant was threatening to exacerbate her already-tenuous condition. Mary was in decidedly ill health and most certainly in need of assistance, so recently Cornelius had hired a "servant girl," essentially a young maid to help alleviate many of his wife's household responsibilities.

Josephine Mumm had come to work for the Murphys back in February, hired to help out around the house as Mary neared the middle of what was clearly a challenging pregnancy. A capable and reliable but sometimes sassy and sharp-tongued girl from the east side – she lived with her widowed mother and younger brothers at 310 Mulberry Street, right in the heart of the still-pastoral Fruit Belt neighborhood – Josephine was eighteen years old, and she'd signed on not only to keep the house in order but also to care for and look after the three Murphy children as well as the coming newborn.

The family's finances, however, were not looking good. Unable to satisfy the mortgage, Cornelius suffered what was undoubtedly a crippling humiliation when the bank foreclosed on their home, forcing him to rent from that same bank the very place they had come to regard as their own. And even this he could not manage, apparently. He was perpetually behind in the rent, and despite measures taken to help offset expenses – the U.S. Census Bureau's 1900 report shows a handful of boarders and lodgers residing there – by the summer of 1902 Cornelius was essentially underwater and seeking more affordable quarters for his family elsewhere in the city.

* * * * * *

Nothing unusual had transpired throughout the day on Tuesday, June 17, 1902.

By late afternoon Cornelius had returned home from the office, and at around 5 p.m. the family sat down to dinner. Josephine served them liver and bacon, along with warmed-over potatoes, bread and butter and some tea. Marian, the second-oldest of the Murphy children and apparently the fussy eater of the family, seemed a bit less than enthused so her mother offered her a bribe: five cents on the condition that she finish everything on her plate. This incentive in place, Josephine would later recall, Marian did exactly that and successfully claimed her five pennies.

Not quite six years old – her birthday was just a month away, on July 18 – little Marian was said to be her father's most favored, the apple of his eye, so to speak. Not quite four feet tall, she was small and petite for her age with a fair complexion, blond hair and piercing blue eyes. The only existing photograph of Marian, captured in a portrait of the Murphy children, shows an absolutely cherubic young thing with a precious face, chipmunk cheeks and a huge mass of curls atop her little head.

In addition to being generally well-liked, the girl was regarded as "naturally bright" by her teachers at nearby Holy Angels Church, where she attended Sunday school classes with her older sister Angela, nearly eight, and her younger brother Leo, almost four. Located just two blocks up West Avenue from her home, where that street intersects with Porter Avenue, the Romanesque-style Catholic convent had been built in 1859, and it stands today as part of the surrounding D'Youville University campus. (Interestingly, had Marian returned there the following year one of her schoolmates would have been a boy named Scott, who was two months younger than herself and lived with his parents in the nearby Allentown neighborhood; the kid would attend only briefly, although he would later rise to world-wide prominence as the celebrated author F. Scott Fitzgerald.)

Anxious to spend her newly-acquired pennies, Marian right away asked for permission to head out to a nearby drug store, a place just around the corner and one block up at the corner of Pennsylvania Street and Plymouth Avenue (this building, at 315 Pennsylvania, is one of many late-nineteenth century buildings which remain standing, giving the neighborhood much of its distinctive Victorian-era flavor). Owned and operated by a gentleman named Edgar Bargar, the place sold ice cream sodas, which Marian loved and knew she could purchase with her coins. After leaving Bargar's she went straight home, arriving just as her father was preparing to head back out.

It was around 6 p.m. when Cornelius left the house, setting out to complete a slew of errands and also to visit with various acquaintances and smoke a few cigars. His wife, for her part, was thoroughly exhausted and completely frayed of nerve. Marian brought her mother some medicine, and as she did the child requested permission to go back outside. No, Mary told her, preferring that she remain indoors for the night, but Marian protested that some of her friends were already out there waiting for her to join them. With this Mary acquiesced, telling her daughter she could go back out but only for a bit.

For the neighborhood kids, gathering outside after dinner was pretty much a nightly ritual. It is said that sometimes as many as ten or twelve youngsters would assemble out there, ready to play and roam until one by one their parents called them back in. Tonight it was just three of Marian's friends – Emma McGinness, Etha Carrick and Hazel Beegle – and anxiously she ran outside to join them, out-fitted in a blue calico sailor-style blouse with white polka dots and little braids about the collar. She had on black stockings and black shoes, and although it was a chilly night she wore neither a hat nor a coat.

These three girls, actually, were nearly twice Marian's age. They all lived right there on that block, and they very kindly included her in all of their playtime activities. Ten-year-old Emma McGinness lived almost all the way down the block at 222 West Avenue, on the op-posite side of the road and just before its intersection with Hudson Street. Etha Carrick, eleven, lived several houses closer at 245, on the Murphys' side. Hazel Beegle, also eleven, lived directly across from them at 256. Although she was a year younger than Etha and Hazel, Emma seems to have been the group's ringleader, so to speak, and breathlessly she led the tribe in their nightly frolic about the neigh-borhood.

At around 8 p.m. Josephine called Marian back in, causing the child to "sulk" and "pout," and in order to evade capture she went charging up the stairs and burrowed beneath a bed. Her mother, far too weak and in no condition to deal with a petulant temper tan-trum, again relented and allowed her daughter to go back out. When Josephine called for her a bit later, though, the girl expressed her dis-pleasure by calling her caretaker nasty names, and before Josephine could stop her she bolted right back out the door. Apprising Mary of this, Josephine requested permission to slap the girl when she finally caught up to her.

"Oh, don't bother," Mary told her. "Let her stay up until her father comes home. She wants to wait up for him."

It wasn't too long before both Etha and Hazel decided to retire for the evening, bidding farewell to Marian and Emma and returning to their respective homes. Emma, however, was not quite ready to call it a night. She had five cents of her own, a nickel given to her by her father, and she knew of a nearby candy store where they could score some pre-bedtime sweets. Marian had never been to or even heard of this place, but with the prospect of candy on the horizon she didn't require too much convincing. Emma also persuaded her to bring along her brother's "wheel" – a popular term for a bicycle at that time – which Marian herself could not ride but the much-older Emma certainly could.

Together they set off, heading down West and crossing over Hudson before coming to a tiny, crooked alleyway that cuts off to the left. Malta Place, as described by one local newspaper, "is an alley about 16 feet wide running in a curve from West Avenue from a point about 200 feet East of Hudson Street around to Maryland Street." Another paper declared it "obscure" and "confusing," a fair assessment judging by the state of the alley today, and yet another cautioned that "grown persons would hesitate to pass through parts of that narrow place." The alley was dotted with little more than a few shacks and a handful of barns, with manure heaps out back and in the fields in between. The place was absolutely desolate and deserted after nightfall, which was fast approaching, but still Marian went willingly as Emma led them up and along the thin, dark lane.

Just over a hundred feet up the alley curves, making a hard right and extending a bit to its terminus at Maryland Street. Another hundred feet past that curve, on the righthand side, stood their destination – a newly-erected residential-type structure at 30 Malta Place, owned by a tailor named Henry Scheuerling whose wife ran a small candy shop there on the premises. Scheuerling would later confirm that the girls had been in there around 8:30 p.m., with Emma and Marian spending just one penny between them and leaving with a stick of gum and four cents change.

Heading back, Marian allowed Emma to ride the bicycle and Emma allowed Marian to hold onto her pennies. Backtracking out of Malta Place the two hung right on West, making their way back up the street in the direction of their homes. Emma's house was just across Hudson, but when the girls reached that point, Emma later reported, Marian took off running ahead toward her own home at the end of the block. Starting after her, Emma said, she watched as Marian passed her house and instead rounded the corner there, turning right and dashing up Pennsylvania Street.

Reaching that spot and finding Marian nowhere in sight, Emma said she rode up and down Pennsylvania, as well as several adjoining streets, in search of her younger playmate. An alternate narrative does exist, incidentally, in which it has been suggested that Emma perhaps had refused to relinquish the "wheel," instead riding ahead and out of sight, leaving her much-younger companion standing at West and Pennsylvania confused and all by herself. Either way, it was at that spot where she had last laid eyes on Marian, and this was later determined to have been at approximately 8:40 p.m.

Emma was still out looking several minutes later when she encountered Etha Carrick, who had gone home nearly a half-hour earlier but was now outside not far from her house. Etha had just seen Marian a few minutes prior, she declared, and Marian had told her she was hiding from Emma. Together she and Emma walked up Pennsylvania to Plymouth, checking inside the drug store there (the one owned by Edgar Bargar, where Marian had purchased an ice cream soda earlier in the evening), but having no luck they decided to turn back and call it an evening. Emma left the bicycle in the Murphys' yard, and the girls went back into their own houses around 9 p.m.

Shortly thereafter Cornelius returned home, where he was alarmed to learn that his youngest daughter had not yet returned for the night. He called her name out in the street, but no response came. With this he summoned Josephine, directing her to go out and search the neighborhood while he did the same. Cornelius, for his part, headed straight back up to Bargar's drug store, but finding it closed and locked up for the night he instead began asking anyone he came across if they might have seen his little child. No one had.

Josephine, meanwhile, ventured out to have a look about the neighborhood, but she didn't get very far. Right outside the house, just steps away at the corner of West and Pennsylvania, she spotted a man she thought to be acting suspiciously. He was of medium height, slimly-built and well-dressed, wearing dark clothes with a white collar, a tie and a slouch hat. Upon her approach, Josephine would later claim, the man came out from beneath the tree he'd been leaning on and rushed right at her, running full-tilt and halfway out into the street before halting abruptly and retreating to his initial station.

This sent Josephine running back into the house, and as she did, she said, the man followed after her. Quickly she locked the door, and peering out the window she could see him standing out front and staring intently back at the Murphy home. He kept this up for about a minute, then returned to the corner and disappeared down Pennsylvania Street. Josephine was positive he had not been there awaiting a streetcar, and at least one local paper would soon suggest that the man may have been a "masher" (per a 2017 article in the online *Collectors Weekly*, this late-eighteenth century term refers to a vain, pompous, foppish type who shamelessly, and often very public-ly, makes passionate advances at unaccompanied women).

It was around midnight when Cornelius returned, empty-handed and without so much as a clue as to what could have happened to his daughter, or where she could possibly be. He and his wife were in the habit of allowing her to play outside unsupervised, but generally she stuck to the yard or at least to the immediate vicinity. She had never ventured further than Niagara Street, he later recalled, which was three blocks to the southwest and well before the Erie Canal, infa-mous for having claimed the lives of small children who had fallen in and perished in its filthy, disease-infested waters.

Marian had been missing for three and a half hours, and as the ter-rible gravity of the situation set in Cornelius knew the police needed to become involved. That pocket of Buffalo's west side fell under the jurisdiction of the tenth precinct, so in mounting distress he rang its stationhouse at 566 Niagara Street, a stately, Victorian-style chateau just three blocks over and one block up from the Murphy residence.

Fully aware of the urgency in play, Cornelius also sat down to tele-phone the local newspapers, anxious to get Marian's description out there and to appeal to the citizenry of the city to help bring his little girl home.

TWO

A Neighborhood Frenzy

The good people of Buffalo, at the dawn of the twentieth century, had a variety of major daily newspapers to choose from – at least seven altogether, in stark and sober contrast to the one they have available to them today.

Two of these papers – the *Buffalo Courier* and the *Buffalo Express* – came out first thing in the morning, while the remaining five – the *Buffalo Evening News*, the *Buffalo Evening Times*, the *Buffalo Enquirer*, the *Buffalo Commercial* and the *Buffalo Review* – all were published in the evening. (A note concerning reproductions made here from these sources: in quoting from the afore-mentioned newspapers, most grammatical irregularities and typographical errors have been preserved for the sake of historical accuracy, as have numerous instances of certain nomenclatures long retired from polite and popular lexicon.)

As the sun came up on the morning of Wednesday, June 18, commuters aboard the city's numerous clanging trolley cars were perusing the morning papers and first taking note of a missing child on the city's west side. The *Courier*, for instance, ran this brief paragraph on page seven:

> When James Murphy, who resides at No. 257 West Avenue, returned to his home shortly after 10 o'clock last night he found that his little 6-year-old daughter Mary was missing. The child took some pennies and went out on the street about 8 o'clock in the evening, supposably to get some candy. While gone her mother, who is in poor health, fell asleep and did not awake until after 9 o'clock to find that Mary had not returned. A search was instituted in the neighborhood, but without avail. The police at No. 10 Station were notified, but up to midnight the child had not been found. The home is about half a mile from any water, hence there is no suspicion that she has been drowned.

It wasn't much in the way of sounding a city-wide alarm, and obviously the reporter got a few key details wrong (Marian's father's name was Cornelius, not James, and the missing girl technically was still five for another month). And with no real urgency conveyed, most readers simply went on about their day without giving the matter a second thought.

At the tenth precinct, meanwhile, its captain, Patrick H. Kilroy, had been put in charge of the official investigation, and right away he'd gone to work assessing what little information police had available to them. As with any missing persons case time was of the essence, and for Kilroy the exigency of the matter was no doubt compounded by the fact that he lived with his own family just over on Seventh Street, five short blocks from the spot where Marian had vanished the night before.

Naturally Kilroy began assigning his best men to the case, and these included Malcolm Cornish, a detective special investigator with fourteen years on the job and a reputation as "one of the ablest men in the department," as someone would later indicate to the *Evening News*. Cornish, along with four other officers and a bicycle patrolman, set out that morning with "orders to search every vacant lot, every vacant house, barn or other building unoccupied in that vicinity."

Their work for the day also included a top-to-bottom search of the Murphy residence, if only to make certain the girl wasn't still inside the home, hiding or hurt and unable to call out for help. Beyond that, the *Courier* noted, empty barns along Plymouth Avenue were being tossed, with officers displaying "an unusual amount of energy" and seeming to "want to do what they could for the child's grief-stricken parents."

Cornelius, for his part, was beginning to express concern that his daughter may have been kidnapped. It certainly seemed a stretch, as he hardly drew the type of salary that would satisfy any worthwhile ransom. Still, the story of Josephine's encounter with a dapper and ominous weirdo right outside his family's home had put him on edge and set his mind to pondering the possibility. "I am afraid my daughter has been kidnaped," he told a man from the *Evening Times* that afternoon. "I don't know how else to explain her disappearance.

Nobody saw her after 8 o'clock and none of the other children saw where she went. This is the neighborhood where all those holdups have been taking place and we can't help fearing that she has fallen into the hands of ruffians who are holding her for a reward. We are following up every clue, and hope that she will turn up today."

Another dreadful possibility lay a little over a half a mile to the southwest, where the Erie Canal, already the site of numerous child fatalities, sat stagnant and indifferent to the peril it posed to careless and unattended youngsters. That seemed unlikely to police, given the distance, but in order to cover all bases Captain Kilroy stationed four additional officers at all points along the canal from Maryland Street to Porter Avenue, a span of roughly four blocks.

Marian's mother and siblings, of course, were devastated and in shock, keeping anxious vigil just outside their home and praying desperately for any word of the little girl's whereabouts. "Loving little girl and boy friends surrounded Mrs. Murphy as she sat on the porch of her home this morning," the *Evening Times* reported, "offering suggestions to help restore the child to its grief-stricken parents." Older kids of the neighborhood – the ones with bicycles, especially – immediately banded together, forming a ragtag sort of task force that went out hunting for any trace of the girl, prowling local backyards and checking out all the nearby gathering spots.

The *Evening Times* reporter who called there found Marian's poor mother appearing "pale and ill and careworn," filled with dread and beginning to think her daughter really had been kidnapped. "Marion was a sweet and loving child and I fear that some person has kidnaped her," she told him. "The child was of a sweet disposition and would talk to any person that came along. I think that somebody kidnaped her while she was sitting in front of her home or enticed her away." If Marian were merely lost the police would have located her by now, she reasoned, adding: "I don't dare go into the house for some reason or other. I have a sort of a dread and want to be out and look for my child."

That afternoon, amidst a gaggle of callers, the Murphy home was visited by a young man who lived nearby and claimed to have some relevant information he wanted to share with the family. Nineteen-year-old Lloyd Van Horn lived with his parents just two blocks away at 288 Maryland Street; his father Guy owned a business downtown, while his mother Mary ran a small shop out of their home selling confectionaries, newspapers, cigars and tobacco. Their home was a very short distance from where Malta Place lets out on its opposite side, and just a few hundred feet up Maryland.

The previous night, Lloyd said, around the time Marian was said to have gone missing, he'd been sitting out on his front steps when he saw a young girl alone and crying in Maryland Street, terribly upset and seemingly lost. Before long, he said, a bigger girl came along and led the child away and out of sight. Boosting his story's credibility was the fact that, unprompted, he'd asked: "Was she a little light-haired girl with a blue polka dot dress?"

This possible sighting on Maryland quickly gave rise to the theory that Marian, after becoming separated from Emma McGinnis, may actually have doubled back, perhaps intending to visit Henry Scheuerling's Malta Place candy shop a second time (she still had Emma's four pennies in her possession). She could easily have then exited at the wrong end of the alley by accident, quickly becoming disoriented and winding up wandering around aimlessly in a weepy panic.

It was soon learned, however, that Lloyd Van Horn and his whole story had been nothing but a complete waste of time, a cruel fabrication thought up by a thoughtless young man who'd "apparently thought it would be a nice thing to have his name in the papers," as the *Courier* later put it. Police began to suspect as much when he failed to come down to the station as requested for an interview; also from the *Courier*: "Although pressed for a statement to the police, he failed to materialize at the stationhouse yesterday to make his statement. The police class him in the 'hot air' category."

What's worse, it was soon learned that Lloyd had actually paid a visit to Scheuerling's candy store on his way to visit the Murphys, learning from its proprietor what the child had been wearing the night before.

* * * * * *

By the next day – Thursday, June 19 – absolutely no progress had been made in any direction, and the *Buffalo Courier* presented its early morning readers with four possible scenarios which may have befallen young Marian Murphy.

The first was that she'd been kidnapped and was being held for ransom, which was doubtful given the family's limited financial means; what's more, no one thus far had made contact to put forth any demands. Another was that she had fallen into the Erie Canal and drowned, and throughout the day calls would develop to begin dragging its polluted waters for any trace of the missing girl's body. The third, far-more-palatable notion was that Marian may have been found and taken in, perhaps by some kindly and oblivious older person who didn't read the papers. The fourth was that she had been "carried away by tramps," as Buffalo had at that time "an unusually large number of suspicious persons of the hobo variety."

The neighborhood, meanwhile, was abuzz with worry, its residents "anxious and alarmed as they seldom have been before in all their lives," the *Buffalo Evening News* reported. "Parents realize that if little Marian Murphy can be stolen or otherwise disappear from a thickly-settled residence district no child is safe." The entire city had taken interest, in fact, and throughout the day hundreds of well-meaning citizens would phone in tips to that publication as well as all the others.

And, for a second day, a steady flow of people came calling at the Murphy residence, each stopping by to offer what little he or she could in the way of comfort to the devastated family. These were, the *Buffalo Review* reported, "people of all degrees and stations in life." The house remained crowded throughout the afternoon, and a good number of those visitors, actually, were newspapermen and police detectives.

Police had been on hand since daybreak, searching underneath all the houses in the immediate vicinity of the Murphy place. "It is thought by some that she may have crawled under a house while at play," the *Courier* explained, "her dress having then been caught in some nails she might have been unable to get out or make herself heard." For going on forty hours now the men of the tenth precinct had been working tirelessly, and their captain, Patrick Kilroy, would boldly state as much to that paper: "I have had my men go into every vacant house, into every alley, and to look into every cellarway or hole into which a person might fall. We are doing everything possible to find the girl and I hope we will succeed."

Police also were fielding any incoming tips, a good many of which were arriving directly to the Murphy home throughout the afternoon. Hazel Beegle, Marian's older playmate from across the street, was now claiming to have heard a young girl scream around 10 p.m. the night her young friend went missing. Sometime in the afternoon another little girl came dashing into the house, breathlessly exclaiming that a friend of hers had spotted Marian five blocks up on Rhode Island Street. This was followed up on right away, however it turned out to be nothing more than an irresponsible bit of schoolkid gossip.

Sometime shortly after noon Captain Kilroy himself appeared at 257 West Avenue, stopping by to assure the Murphy family that his men were leaving no stone unturned in their relentless quest to find the missing child. Around that time someone came by to report a possible Marian sighting on Herkimer Street, a mile and a half to the north, where a man in a grocery store had witnessed a young girl being tugged up the road, crying and protesting, by two strange women dressed in black on the night Marian had gone missing. Kilroy dispatched a bicycle patrolman to follow up at once, but it turned out the timeline didn't quite comport and that theory also fell apart within an hour.

Another lead developed a short while later when the home was visited by a man named Daniel Burns, a contractor who lived with his family a couple blocks away at 41 Fargo Avenue. His eight-year-old daughter Montrose, he said, was peripherally acquainted with Marian, and the previous night, after overhearing her parents discuss the girl's disappearance, she'd piped up and announced to them the following: "I know that little girl. I saw her in Fargo Park last night and she asked me to go to the Front with her, but I told her it was too late. She had on a blue dress and was bareheaded." This, the

Evening News stated, had been "along toward dark on the evening [Marian had] disappeared."

The Front, as it was called back then, was a fifty-acre public park located seven blocks away toward the foot of Porter Avenue. Designed by Frederick Law Olmsted as part of Buffalo's linked parks system, it occupied a bluff overlooking the spot where Lake Erie converges with the Niagara River, and at its eastern end there was a large play area that drew youngsters from all over that part of the city. Now called Front Park, this once-open and inviting space has since been greatly diminished, interrupted by the I-190 and paved over by its various access roads and onramps. At that time, however, the spot was still a "magnet that [drew] thousands of children there every week, every evening," the *Buffalo Evening Times* wrote, and Marian herself was no stranger to its giant playground and wide-open running spaces.

Cornelius was adamant that his daughter had never wandered quite that far on her own, but Burns' story was bolstered by another tip that came in around that time, this one placing Marian at the Front a little later that same evening. A local schoolteacher, another West Avenue resident named Miss Hare, was said to have seen a young girl answering Marian's description sitting alone on a stone there, and according to the *Evening News* this had been "late on Tuesday evening." The *Review*, however, soon learned that that sighting had been another bust, with Miss Hare explaining that "a chance remark of hers had been magnified. She had indeed seen a child, but the description did not tally."

A little before 1 p.m. a mail carrier arrived, delivering a piece of correspondence that the *Courier* found amusing enough to report on: "The letter was an anonymous one and advised Mr. and Mrs.

Murphy to go to a trance medium on East Eagle Street not far from Michigan Street. The letter assured the Murphys that the trance medium would be able to tell them where their daughter could be found." That evening, according to the *Courier*, that medium was in fact called upon but found to be woefully lacking in the credibility department: "A well-meaning neighbor consulted her. 'The rippling, silvery waters,' 'the cars,' and about everything that the average human being would guess in such a case were mentioned. No stock is taken in this at all."

Late that afternoon police heard from William Mahoney, a fourteen-year-old neighborhood kid who lived several blocks from the Murphys over on Seventh Street (the papers all gave his address as 427, although the 1902 Buffalo City Directory lists the Mahoney residence at 769). Willie, as he was called, said he was familiar with Marian from seeing her around the Front, and he too had a story to tell about the night she'd gone missing.

He'd been on his way home from the Front, he said, walking down Plymouth Avenue as it neared Pennsylvania Street, when a familiar-looking girl came rounding that corner and went running up Plymouth toward Hudson Street. This, William said, had been at around 8:45 p.m., and he was certain of the time because he had a 9 p.m. curfew and just minutes earlier he'd asked a man to check his watch. Continuing on Pennsylvania, the kid said, a block up at West Avenue he'd encountered Emma McGinness and Etha Carrick, who were out looking for Marian themselves, and he had pointed them in the right direction.

He was certain it had been her, William told Captain Kilroy. "Oh, I knew it was her all right, because she used to come over on the lot and watch us play ball," he said. "I knew her name was Murphy, because I used to hear the fellows say: 'Look out "Murph," you'll get hurt.'" It sure seemed like a solid lead, but there was one big problem - neither Emma nor Etha nor any of Marian's other playmates could confirm speaking with the Mahoney kid on the evening in question. What's more, William was unable to identify Marian in a series of photographs shown to him by police, and within a day or so his story also would be discredited and wholly dismissed.

* * * * * *

Of the countless people who came by that day, however, most did so to pay their solemn respects, and to sit with Mary Murphy awhile and share in her unimaginable worry.

And, as sympathizing neighbors gathered there speculating as to what may have happened to young Marian, an offhand remark caught Cornelius's attention and really got him thinking. Everyone from blocks around, it seemed, had stopped by to offer up their prayers and consolation, all with the exception of one family in particular.

Albert and Clara Gibbs lived just across the street and on the corner, in a huge house at 277 Pennsylvania Street (so listed because its front faces Pennsylvania, while the side yard is on West Avenue facing the Murphy home). Both Albert and Clara each were independently wealthy, and they were merely renting a space in the enormous, turreted (still-standing) house with their two young children. Their daughter Helene had been a steady playmate of Marian's since they'd moved there two weeks earlier – Clara would later state that she herself had grown quite fond of Marian, having even bought the girl a dress on one occasion – however no one from their household had been by to check on the family or to show even the slightest measure of support.

This prompted Cornelius to recall an incident a week earlier involving the Gibbs' missing dog, which had caused something of a neighborhood stir when Clara accused Josephine Mumm, the Murphys' servant girl, of stealing the pooch and harboring it back at her own home. The couple was visibly eccentric, and what's more their landlady, Elizabeth Gaudy, had been heard to remark that "they were elegantly dressed, were very wealthy, and [they] were very mysterious about things," according to the *Buffalo Review*.

This put his Irish thoughts to racing, and before long Cornelius was out the door and charging across the street, headed for the house on the corner and hell-bent on getting some answers. Clara came to the door and was quickly joined by her husband, and right away the two of them were met with a barrage of accusing and interrogative questions. Noticing that it was Clara who supplied most of the answers, Cornelius made a curt remark about her being "the man of the house" and apparently things only heated up from there. Before slamming the door in his face, Cornelius told a *Buffalo Courier* reporter, the woman had turned to him and hissed: "You know where your child is; you will find her."

Crossing back over West and walking toward his home, Cornelius appeared to that same reporter to be fuming mad and "almost beyond control." Loudly he told him, and all the other reporters within earshot, about the strange and confusing remark the infuriatingly uncooperative woman had just made. Eventually a police officer arrived, a patrolman named McGrady, and although Cornelius was loudly calling for the couple's arrest McGrady managed to calm him down and get him to go back inside his house. Cornelius was "of erratic temperament" to begin with, the *Courier* acknowledged, but the unbearable stress of his daughter's disappearance "has so preyed upon his mind that at times he has not full control of himself."

A short while later the *Courier* man spoke with Clara Gibbs, who initially declined to comment but finally relented and started chattering away, eventually coming clean about her reason for wanting to keep her family out of the whole frightening affair. "I will admit," she confessed, "that there is a possibility of the Murphy girl having been taken in mistake for my little girl." This was a stunning remark, as it painted a salacious picture that would fairly leap off the front page in the form of headline news – Marian Murphy may have been kidnapped *by mistake*, her abductor having confused her for another little girl who lived across the way.

Clara continued: "There is one person – I don't want to do him an injustice – who might have attempted to steal my child. I do not think this person would be mean enough to do this, though, and I feel that I am doing him an injustice, although I must confess that he has blackmailed me and threatened me." She could divulge nothing more than that, Clara flatly insisted, before slyly leaning toward her interviewer and allowing, in a hushed whisper, that she was speaking of her own brother.

Her brother's name was Alonzo J. Whiteman, and he enjoyed an unusual sort of notoriety at the time, known across the country as an expert conman, swindler and forger. Regarded as "one of the most skillful forgers and con men in the country," according to a 2022 article in the online *MinnPost*, Alonzo had been born in 1861 to a wealthy family in Dansville, New York, where he had known "a youth of wealth, privilege, and education," followed by "a young adulthood of dazzling attainment." Upon graduating Hamilton College he'd gone on to complete a year of law school at Columbia University, then relocating to Duluth, Minnesota, where he established a real estate firm, a bank and a name for himself in local politics. In 1886 he'd been elected Duluth's mayor, later becoming the youngest member to ever serve in the Minnesota Senate.

Alonzo's unravelling, it was said, stemmed from his 1890 defeat in a three-way congressional race, and the decade that followed was marked by compulsive gambling, massive debt, check forgery and countless arrests across the country. His modus operandi, as it were, was to arrive in a new city and open a series of bank accounts under an assumed name, spending wildly and dashing out of town before the checks came bouncing back. Most recently he had been arrested for the twenty-second time after forging a check at the Hotel Navarre in New York City, and although he'd received a two-and-a-half-year prison sentence it had been overturned on appeal and presently Lon (as he was sometimes called) was laying low back in Dansville.

By now, though, Lon Whiteman was claiming to have turned over a new leaf and he was a regular at his local Methodist church, often using his sly and silvery tongue to address the congregation there. "In 1902 Whiteman took a break from crime to set himself up as a Methodist preacher in and around Dansville," the *MinnPost* noted, wryly adding that "that career did not last long." He most likely found a life of crime to be simpler and more lucrative, and all told Whiteman would go on to be arrested nearly fifty times, always onto the next big con but rarely spending so much as a night in jail despite his over-the-top brazenness.

The summer of 1902, however, found him living with his mother in Dansville, financially underwater and heavily engaged in a lawsuit against his sister over the estate of their late father Reuben, who had died back in 1888. Clara, he alleged, had withheld some portion of the money he was entitled to, and lately he had been hounding her relentlessly, repeatedly requesting cash advances and ultimately demanding she pay him a large settlement outright.

Three weeks earlier, Clara told a *Review* reporter, her brother had tracked her down in Detroit and "demanded money not stating a definite sum, but decreasing as she refused, until at last he flatly asked for 'only $2,500.'" She had denied him even that amount, Clara said, to which he'd replied that he would find "a way to put her on the bum and make her crawl." This, she told the *Buffalo Evening News*, had caused her to fear for the safety of her family: "Dire threats were made. I have been warned since to keep watch of my two children. I have been told they might be kidnaped." From the *Review*: "Some few days ago Mrs. Gibbs was warned by a friend whom she believed to have seen her brother, to be very careful of her little girl, as there was danger hovering over her."

That evening Clara was summoned to Buffalo Police Department headquarters, then located all the way downtown on the Terrace, a blocks-long promenade and Buffalo's first-ever public assembly space. Prior to the 1870s, before Frederick Law Olmsted's extensive parks system linked one side of the city to the other, the Terrace had been Buffalo's main outdoor gathering spot. By the turn of the century, though, numerous vital businesses had sprung up along its lower perimeter, including one of the busiest commuter train stations in the country, making the strip a bustling hive of downtown activity (this part of the Terrace technically still exists, although it does so amidst a tangle of concrete pillars and noisy overpasses, with all traces of its former self long since obliterated to accommodate the I-190 and the northern end of the Skyway).

Built back in 1884, the huge and imposing police station occupied basically a small city block, stretching along the Terrace between Erie and West Seneca Streets and bordered to the east by Franklin Street. Inside she met with Superintendent of Police William S. Bull, a weathered, stone-faced former Army general with thinning white hair and a prominent handlebar mustache, the head of the department since 1894. Most recently he had overseen the case against the assassin Leon Czolgosz, whose trial for the murder of President William McKinley had concluded nine months earlier with a successful conviction, the killer then sentenced to death via electrocution at Auburn Prison.

Superintendent Bull was a storied figure in local law enforcement, and right away he took to the kidnapping theory, sending word for police in nearby cities to be on the lookout for Lon Whiteman, either in the presence of a five-year-old child or otherwise. He'd been convinced, the *Evening News* reported, by one detail in particular. "The two children, it is said, were dressed almost exactly alike," that paper wrote, referring to the night of Marian's vanishing. "Marian wore a blue calico print sailor suit, with white polka-dots. Helene Gibbs wore a dress of the same cut and size. It was of blue without the polka-dots."

And while the city's top cop was more or less sold on the whole kidnapping angle, Clara herself had already thought things through and changed her mind completely. While at headquarters she also met with Malcolm Cornish, veteran detective special investigator from the tenth precinct, who drew from her the following statement, per the *Evening News*:

"When I first heard of the disappearance of the Murphy child the thought that first occurred to me was, could my brother have had anything to do with it? I thought for the moment that perhaps he might have attempted to carry off Helene and got the Murphy child by mistake. But the absurdity of the supposition was apparent at once. In the first place my brother does not know we are in Buffalo. We threw him off the track completely when we left Detroit and we have lived here so quietly for the express purpose of eluding him, that he simply could not have discovered our present location.

"In the second place he is not a man who would resort to any such device either to obtain money or for revenge. And in the third place he would take good care to assure himself he had the right child if he undertook any kidnaping. This Murphy child was fair and had light hair. Helene is as dark as a Gypsy. If my brother undertook to do any kidnaping he would not go farther than the nearest lamppost before finding out he had a white-headed, blue-eyed child instead of a dark-eyed, dark-haired one like Helene. I am satisfied he had nothing to do with it."

Superintendent Bull may have remained dedicated to the kidnapping angle, but Detective Cornish and most of the others had already grown doubtful of the notion, having telegrammed authorities in Dansville and learned that Whiteman hadn't left that city in weeks. "There is," Captain Kilroy assured the *Evening News*, as well as any other paper that asked, "absolutely nothing to it."

THREE

Dead Ends

The following morning began down at the canal, the general consensus amongst detectives now being that, in all likelihood, Marian Murphy had wandered the seven blocks from her home, fallen in and drowned. Two crew members of the police patrol boat Governor Morton were dispatched to check from Hudson Street to Porter Avenue, heading out in a pair of smaller rowboats to comb the canal's gross and rancid waters with hooks and grappling irons.

It was Friday, June 20, and Marian had not been seen in over sixty hours. And finally, the *Buffalo Evening Times* reported, Albert and Clara Gibbs did drop by the Murphys' house to offer their support, and also to assure the couple that Clara's brother could not have been involved in any way. "This morning Mr. and Mrs. Gibbs called at the home of the Murphys and said they would do all in their power to help find the missing girl," the *Evening Times* wrote. "They told Mrs.

Murphy not to put any stock in the rumor that Whiteman might have had something to do with the child's disappearance." Mary Murphy, however, remained unconvinced. "Until I hear and know definitely that Whiteman had nothing to do with Marian's disappearance I shall be inclined to believe there is something in the rumor that he might have been connected with it," she stated flatly.

As for Cornelius, the *Buffalo Review* would provide its readers with this helpful update regarding his overall well-being: "An unfortunate feature of this case is that Cornelius Murphy, the child's father, who has suffered previously from temporary derangements, is rapidly entering an unfortunate nervous state, and the family is greatly alarmed for his health. The strain has been very heavy upon him and he is falling under it."

With growing public interest and the case beginning to draw national attention, police still were fielding incoming tips and reports concerning the night Marian had gone missing. The next one rolled in that afternoon, and it was from a gentleman named Isaac Bakker, a 44-year-old boatbuilder who owned and operated a small boatyard down at the foot of Jersey Street, where he lived with his wife Nettie and their six children. His kids had been outside playing that Tuesday night, Baker claimed, when they'd seen something in the water that had given them all a scare, and which also might lend credence to the currently-favored drowning theory.

They'd been playing on a raft out front of the family's boatyard, and twelve-year-old Albert Baker had been the first to spot it. "There's a dead dog in the water," he'd called out to his siblings, adding, "let's see if we can hit it with a stone." From the *Evening Times*: "When he first saw the floating object it was some distance above the raft, floating some distance out. It quickly neared them and the children saw a tiny head with hair on it and once, when an eddy in the canal twisted the object about, they saw what they supposed to be a human face. They were almost speechless with fright and quit throwing stones and Albert said: 'That isn't a dog, it's a body, someone's been drowned. Don't throw any more stones.'" This, the Baker kids recalled, had happened at around 8:30 p.m., and police would continue dragging the canal for the remainder of the day.

That afternoon, right around 2 p.m., Cornelius took a look outside and noticed something odd. It was Albert Gibbs, and he was loading some traveling trunks into a closed carriage that was waiting out front by the curb. With him was his eight-year-old son, Helene's older brother Reginald, and as their hired horse drove off Cornelius correctly intuited that something clandestine was afoot. He and other "members of the Murphy family" – the *Buffalo Courier* did not specify which ones – quickly hopped onto bicycles and began trailing after them, following surreptitiously behind the carriage as it made its way up Pennsylvania Street to what is now called Symphony Circle.

From there the party went north up Richmond Avenue, turning right onto Summer Street and then left on Ashland Avenue, drawing to a halt less than a block up from that intersection. From a distance Cornelius and company watched as the Gibbs males were joined by Clara and Helene, their carriage then turning around and doubling back toward Summer, cutting over to Delaware Avenue and heading downtown. When finally the family alighted it was at the Cleveland & Buffalo Transit Company docks at the foot of Illinois Street, right along the Buffalo River, where they hauled their luggage aboard a grand overnight passenger steamer called the SS *Western States*.

Leaving their trunks and their children safely onboard, the *Cou-*

rier reported, Albert and Clara then stepped back off the ship and "went about the city," as their vessel was not set to depart for some time yet. Upon the couple's return they were met by a reporter from that paper, who inquired about the family's sudden departure and asked if they were headed back to Detroit. "No significance at all," Clara assured him, "can be attached to our leaving. Oh, yes, in fact we have intended to go [to Detroit] for four or five days. Mr. Gibbs was thinking of going yesterday ahead of me, but we decided it would be better to all leave together."

When asked about her brother Lon's possible involvement in the disappearance of Marian Murphy, or about his efforts to extort her the last time she visited that city, Clara replied that she had "nothing further to say than I said yesterday, I think that covers it all." Then, on second thought, she added: "I'm awfully sorry I told you of my suspicions yesterday; it has brought such unpleasant notoriety upon us, but what's done can't be undone." With that the family Gibbs quit Buffalo, although the inevitable cloud of suspicion would linger on in light of the Lon Whiteman rumor.

That afternoon, however, the local papers began hearing from the man himself, and he was rather indignant about the fact that they'd all been running stories insinuating he'd been involved in this ghastly Murphy girl business. One such telegram went to the *Evening Times*, which saw fit to reprint his remarks in full:

> City Editor, Buffalo TIMES:
> The report that I have had anything to do with kidnaping the Murphy child or attempting to kidnap the Gibbs child is too ridiculous to require a denial from me. The differences existing between my sister, Mrs. Gibbs, and myself

will be aired in court in due time. I have no case to try in the newspapers. I went to Detroit three weeks ago at the earnest request of Mrs. Gibbs and at her expense. I made no demand on her for money, nor have I ever blackmailed her. Mrs. Gibbs is in possession of $100,000 which rightfully belongs to me and to my creditors and she has secretly done everything she could to have me sent to prison. But I have never spent a day in a penitentiary or State prison, and I never will. I have not been away from Dansville in the last ten days and have been here all the time since last October.

A.J. Whiteman.

In truth, and despite the newspapers' sensational front-page stories about a renown out-of-town swindler possibly swooping through and snatching up a child, police generally regarded the theory as downright preposterous. Detectives "never for a minute" truly suspected Alonzo Whiteman, the *Evening Times* reported, allowing that right away they'd all essentially "characterized the story as nonsense."

And so, that paper ruminated, "another day passes without any clue as to the whereabouts of Marian Murphy, whether she is in the hands of kidnapers; whether she is at the bottom of the canal or whether she is in the hands of persons who know nothing about the efforts being made to find her."

* * * * * *

The next day was Saturday, June 21. For Mary Murphy, the vanished girl's shocked and devastated mother, very little had changed since her daughter had gone missing more than three days earlier. Most of the woman's time was spent "seated in a little low rocking chair where she could command a view of the steps and see who came and went," the *Buffalo Courier* reported, just as she had all day yesterday afternoon, and "the worst, to her, would be relief compared with the mortal agony she suffers in the suspense."

Her poor, beleaguered face, it was noted, now bore "a careworn look," with "eyes that had become sunken" with sleeplessness and the unbearable stress of not knowing. Mary was being attended to by a local physician, a Dr. William J. O'Donnell, who declared her to be "on the verge of nervous collapse" and in desperate need of respite from the parade of callers who continued to stop by under various pretenses. "Mrs. Murphy is really in a serious condition," he told the *Courier*, "and [she] requires the utmost quiet to restore her nervous system, which is nearly wrecked from the severe strain she has been under."

To help alleviate that stress Dr. O'Donnell was prescribing her valerian, a plant-based remedy physicians have been turning to for centuries, known to alleviate the more severe symptoms of insomnia and anxiety. Today, in the age of Valium and Xanax and so forth, valerian is regarded as little more than a mild sedative and sleep aid. In great enough quantities, though, Marian's mother found that it did take the edge off to some degree, and "this is all that kept her from a complete nervous breakdown after the child was lost," the *Courier* reported. "I just manage to keep myself deadened with the stuff," she told that paper. "When I find that I am able to think quickly and know full well the import of everything, I dose myself with this stuff.

It is all that has kept me up. I try to be heroic for Mr. Murphy's sake. I must set him an example."

But her maternal torment, she confessed, was truly debilitating and nearly without relent: "At night I hear my little one cry. One minute I can feel her little warm body nestled close to mine; another minute it all flits across my mind, these events of four days. I can hear a carriage stop. I know that someone has got out. Can it be that my child is being returned? Is it that someone knows my mental anguish and is relieving me of my trouble. Then, as I lay trying to sleep, with only a measure of success, the noise ceases; no child comes, and I am left to go through with the torture again. If I could only find my little child!"

With no real progress being made by police, Cornelius already had decided that it fell to him to do something proactive in the name of getting his little girl back. The morning papers, then, ran the following notice, arranged for by Cornelius sometime the previous day: "On behalf of friends who are able, which I am not, I desire to make the following offer of reward for the recovery of my child, Marian, six years of age, with light hair and blue eyes, dressed in blue polka dot dress, $1,000 (one thousand dollars), for the return of the child absolutely unharmed."

Predictably, this brought about a flood of incoming correspondence from all over the city, with complete strangers sending in far-fetched tips and well-meaning advice, although much of it far too kooky for police to take seriously. A letter arrived that morning, for instance, from a woman on North Pearl Street suggesting the Murphys consult Dr. Frank O. Matthews, a local physician, surgeon, lecturer, professor and nationally-renown clairvoyant "who could probably trace your girl." He'd had, the woman claimed, considerable success in this arena, and he was held in the highest esteem by members of the city's most respectable social set.

Cornelius, being Catholic, didn't go in for any of that blasphemous business, although the *Buffalo Evening Times* did take the liberty of dispatching a reporter to visit Dr. Matthews at his home at 879 Main Street. "Watch the Gibbses," was the man's statement, and he issued it in no uncertain terms. "I am confident that the Gibbses know about the missing child and I was so confident of it yesterday that I was on the point of calling up Supt. Bull and requesting him to search the house where the Gibbses were stopping. They should not have been allowed to depart without being thoroughly examined. They should be traced and watched, for they may know about the child."

Another, similar card arrived along with it, this one recommending the family consult a Mrs. Smith, a charming and gifted elderly lady living at 105 North Street, who surely would be able to divine the location of the missing child. "I can't do anything of the sort," Mrs. Smith instead told the *Evening Times*. "But I believe that the body of the little girl will be found in the canal."

Soon there was an unannounced visitor at the door, "a young man, apparently a foreigner, for his accent was very peculiar and his make-up very strange," the *Evening Times* noted. His name, he said, was Arthur Seraydorian (Arabic, most likely), and he had taken a great interest in the case. He then handed Cornelius an article he'd clipped about a little girl found drowned all the way down in Long Island. She'd had auburn-colored hair, though, and dejectedly Cornelius explained that "little Marian was more like a white haired child than red-haired."

That afternoon another caller dropped by – "an elegantly dressed woman," according to the *Evening Times*, "apparently a woman of refinement and means" – and she too wanted to recommend a clairvoyant, an East Eagle Street medium whose services were "said to be marvelous." When visited by that paper, however, the fortune-teller "declined to say anything about the case, although admitting that the child would not be returned unharmed."

It would be another disappointing day spent running down dead-end leads and coming up empty. Notably, and with so little of substance to work with, as much investigative work was being done by the local newspapers as it was by detectives, who had searched high and low but made astonishingly little progress, although certainly not for lack of trying.

From that night's edition of the *Buffalo Evening News*: "Every empty house and building, every vacant lot, every bit of shrubbery or tuft of grass that might hide a child's body, has been repeatedly searched for several blocks about the home of Cornelius Murphy, without result. The canal has been dragged from Hudson street to Porter avenue with similar futility. The Police Department has given the mystery its best ability, but the astounding fact remains that a 6-year-old child disappeared within a block of her home early in the evening and nothing has been found to disclose the manner of her taking off."

* * * * * *

The next several days went by much the same way, with vague leads turning up and then crumbling instantly under the weight of any real scrutiny.

The following day, Sunday, a rumor developed concerning a local man named Louis Tolinski, whom the *Buffalo Evening Times* referred to as an "itinerant tailor," seemingly a hobo-type who resorted to plying his one-time trade only when absolutely necessary. A mainstay in the adjacent Allentown neighborhood, the *Buffalo Evening News* reported that Tolinski was "well-known by the police, having done several odd jobs for patrolmen."

He had also done odd jobs for Cornelius Murphy, occasionally repairing his clothes and frequently dropping by the Murphy home looking for food, money or other work. "The children in the neighborhood used to know him very well and all called him 'Louis,' or 'Lou-e-e,'" the *Evening Times* wrote, although Cornelius recently had banned him from coming around after the man had asked Mrs. Murphy for a kiss. Now folks were saying Tolinski hadn't been seen around all the previous week, and Cornelius found that highly suspicious.

First thing the next morning - Monday, June 23 - police followed up on this concern, and right away they tracked Tolinski down at the Erie County Almshouse, several miles north of the city near the intersection of Main Street and Bailey Avenue (that building, today, is part of the University of Buffalo's South Campus, called Hayes Hall and home to its School of Architecture and Planning). "Tolinski was located at the Almshouse today by the police," the *Evening News* reported that afternoon. "He was surprised to hear of the child's disappearance and said he knew absolutely nothing as to her whereabouts. The police credit his story."

But with police constantly reporting back empty-handed, and with the local papers all competing heavily for the city's readership, a narrative of some sort had to be driven forth. The *Evening Times*, for its part, chose to go with police incompetence. That evening, under a brutal headline reading "Police Give Up Hope Of Finding Missing

Child," the paper fairly eviscerated the department's lack of progress, accusing its men of dithering and charging them with sluggishness and even outright ineptitude.

"While hundreds of friends and sympathizers are doing all they can to aid in solving the mystery attending the disappearance of little Marian Murphy," that paper proclaimed, "the police are doing practically nothing, and the inactivity or incompetency of the police in this matter, a matter in which not only the Murphys but the entire population of this community is keenly interested, is causing much comment. It was stated today that the police propose to abandon the case entirely after today, for what reason can not be explained, the only excuse being given is that the police have done all they could to fathom the mystery. But have the police done anything of the kind? There is evidence that the police have not done one half they should have done in the matter."

Pointing specifically to what it called the "half-hearted" manner in which authorities had dragged the canal, the *Evening Times* also called out the glaring lack of resources which had been devoted to the search. "Instead of having the crew of the steam yacht 'Morton' do the dragging," the paper wrote, "two men with a grapnel were detailed in a rowboat, to traverse the length and breadth of the canal, from Maryland Street to Black Rock. This work, wholly unsatisfactory as it was, was dropped on Saturday, and now it is stated on police authority, that the case is to be dropped altogether."

* * * * * *

That last part – the part about police planning to abandon the case outright for lack of any solid leads or developments – was categorically untrue.

Early the next morning, in fact, members of the tenth precinct were out conducting a painstakingly thorough examination of Malta Place, the brief and spooky alleyway just over a block from the Murphy residence, where Marian had gone for candy the night she'd vanished into thin air. It was Tuesday, June 24, and that evening would mark one full week since the girl's baffling disappearance.

The hunt was led by Detective Malcolm Cornish, who had fixed his attention on the small vacant house behind 20 Malta Place, three lots away from Henry Scheuerling's candy shop, as an unoccupied structure – particularly one less than two blocks from a victim's home – would be an ideal spot to conceal the body of a smuggled child. The house, which had been empty for over a year, was entered by Cornish and a detective named O'Grady, as well as a reporter from the (much friendlier) *Buffalo Evening News*, who wrote that a thorough search was conducted but once again nothing of value was learned or discovered.

Having lost all confidence in the Buffalo Police Department, however, the *Buffalo Evening Times* was hardly content to sit around waiting on that agency to bring its readership some breaking news. As such, it dispatched a staff reporter named John S.V. Bowen to poke around the neighborhood, and to talk with residents and see what new information he could dig up. Quite naturally Bowen dropped by the Murphy place straightaway, speaking with Marian's parents and questioning them at length regarding the little girl's habits, her playmates and her usual routines.

There were two places, Cornelius told him, that Marian frequented which had not been followed up on by police. The first was yet another candy shop, this one just around the corner at 281 Hudson Street and owned by a man named Joseph Barone, whom the paper noted had "a clear, honest look" and didn't seem to be involved in any way. The other was a house two doors down from Barone's, a "Chinese laundry" at 285 Hudson where Cornelius occasionally sent his clothes to be washed and folded. Mary concurred, adding that Marian and the other neighborhood kids often gathered to play right there in front of the small, rickety establishment.

Its proprietor was a man named Charley We, a Chinese immigrant who appeared "badly scared," the *Evening Times* wrote, when Bowen came calling at his establishment a little later that morning, a reporter from another paper, the *Buffalo Commercial*, tagging along to piggyback off his scoop. "Are you looking for some China boys?" he asked nervously as the newspapermen came barging in, likely assuming they were authorities there to check for illegal immigrants being housed on the premises. "We was probably of the impression," the *Evening Times* later reflected (with no discernable trace of shame), "that the searchers were officers, as he made no resistance."

"Upstairs," that paper wrote, "the reporter found a garret, with the small door leading to it nailed tight. The nails were extricated and in a remote corner of the attic room there was a suspicious bundle. This was examined by climbing into the garret, but was found to contain only rubbish. Every part of the place where the body of the child could possibly be secreted, was explored and examined even the door beneath the wash-sink being forced apart for this purpose. The yard and the ground beneath the place was examined and no fresh marks of excavation were to be found."

"And," the *Evening Times* continued, "Charley We states that the police did not search his place as they should have done, if they were determined to investigate the case thoroughly." The intent, it would seem, was to shame the police into ramping up their investigatory efforts, despite the department's being at what was essentially a dead end with regards to this frustrating and troublesome case.

But by the week's end nothing further had developed, and Friday's late afternoon edition of the *Buffalo Review* fairly summarized the grim reality of the situation. "The search for Marian Murphy is at a standstill," it declared. "The police have done everything that they can think of and the family has forced every means to the limit in an effort to discover some trace of the missing child."

FOUR

"Her Little Soul's In Heaven"

It was shortly before 9 p.m. on Friday, June 27, when the telephone rang at the sixth precinct stationhouse.

Located at 1444 Main Street, the station serviced Buffalo's Cold Springs neighborhood and was two miles northeast of the tenth precinct, where the search for Marian Murphy was still underway but quickly running out of steam.

Picking up, the desk sergeant on duty was greeted by the voice of George Troup, the superintendent of nearby Forest Lawn Cemetery, who was calling from the closest saloon, one kept by a man named John Ambrose at 1842 Main. He'd gone running there to use the telephone, Troup explained, after his son and another cemetery employee reported to him that they had just discovered the remains of a very young child in a small body of water by the graveyard's western gate. There was speculation, he added, that it may very well be the missing Murphy girl.

Right away the desk sergeant there made contact with the tenth precinct, alerting its captain, Patrick Kilroy, to the discovery at Forest Lawn and letting him know of the tenth's potential interest in the matter. Right away a county undertaker wagon was dispatched, and Kilroy had lead detective Malcolm Cornish head up to the cemetery as well in order to examine the body, and to take charge of the crime scene if appropriate.

Forest Lawn Cemetery, today, is the city of Buffalo's premier and most exclusive burial spot, its 269 acres comprised of rolling hills, walking paths, countless trees and several distinct bodies of water. Back in 1902 those grounds were not quite as expansive – just about two hundred acres, at that point – but the place was every bit as grand and majestic, having come a long way since its official opening a half-century earlier.

George Troup had become superintendent in 1880, back when the place was still called Buffalo City Cemetery, and it was under his leadership that the space had really blossomed and taken shape. "When Mr. Troup took charge of Forest Lawn it was undeveloped and only a small portion of the extensive lands was utilized for burials," the *Buffalo Evening News* would write years later on the occasion of the man's retirement in 1913. "Acres of hard clay soil and insect-eaten trees were practically all that Mr. Troup had out of which to develop and to produce what is now admitted by land scape architects, by funeral directors, and by thousands of visitors to Buffalo to be one of the most beautiful and best planned cemeteries in this country."

Its grounds butted right up against Delaware Park, designed and laid out three decades earlier by Frederick Law Olmsted and Calvert Vaux, and between those two properties Buffalo's citizenry had at its disposal an impressively serene and rural experience right in the middle of what was then the country's eighth-largest city. Bordered to the north by the park, the cemetery stretches west-to-east between Delaware Avenue and Main Street, extending as far south as West Delevan Avenue. The superintendent's quarters were located just inside the Main Street gate, a few hundred yards north of West Delevan, and upon learning of the discovery Troup had gone dashing over to a saloon at that intersection's southwest corner to telephone the police.

He then rejoined the boys and the body on the muddy banks of Swan Lake, the tiny pool of standing water which had just coughed up the young girl's cadaver, the three of them peering at the poor thing in overwhelming sadness while awaiting an undertaker's vehicle. Just a stone's throw from that spot people were riding and driving by on Delaware Avenue, a wrought iron fence the only thing separating all this traffic from the quiet and heavily-treed cemetery grounds, which sat eerily desolate and quiet after sundown. (Swan Lake, today, is long gone, filled in in the late 1950s after its eventual stagnation led to concerns over sewage contamination; in 2017, however, area preservationists began restoring the spot to its former condition, recreating a spring-fed wetland area more or less in the footprint of the original pond.)

Eventually a wagon came, and the deceased girl's remains were removed to the morgue downtown.

* * * * * *

The Erie County Morgue stood at 241 Terrace, just a five-minute walk up from police headquarters, several steps north of the Terrace's intersection with Church Street.

Captain Kilroy was on his way there, and Detective Cornish also was en route, having arrived up at Forest Lawn Cemetery only after the body had been hauled off. A detective named George Palmer, also of the tenth precinct, had been working the case alongside Cornish from day one, and he was summoned to meet them there as well.

Kilroy had also notified Police Superintendent William Bull at headquarters downtown, and Bull promptly went into conference with his second-in-command. Chief of Detectives Patrick V. Cusack was a 63-year-old Irish-born veteran of the city's police force, recently named assistant superintendent of police, and he happened to live at 636 West Avenue, just five blocks up from the Murphys. Certainly the case had his utmost attention, and between Cusack and Bull the decision was made to send one of their own men, Detective Sergeant Hugh Kennedy, down to the morgue as well.

The Erie County Medical Examiner, at the time, was Earl G. Danser, a 44-year-old graduate of the University of Buffalo's College of Medicine, who had been elected the city's coroner just the year before. Less than four months into his term, however, the state legislature abolished that office and replaced it with one of medical examiner, naming Danser to that position. Noted for his meticulous and scientific methodology, Danser lived in nearby Cheektowaga and he belonged to a handful of area fraternal organizations (he was a prominent local Freemason, and also a member in good standing of the Independent Order of Odd Fellows).

The body was wheeled in on a moveable slab, and soon Dr. Danser's assistant arrived. Dr. John D. Howland was a physician with a practice over on Michigan Street, and as deputy medical examiner he was on hand to witness and participate in the initial examination of the girl's found remains. Those lie bundled up in front of them – wrapped in newspaper and cloth and all tied up with rope – and after a solemn moment the ropes were cut and the rank bundle opened up.

The rope about the outside of the parcel, Captain Kilroy later stated, was "a heavy twine, for the most part," although it also has been described as most closely resembling a length of clothesline. The body itself had been wrapped up in newspaper, and that had been enfolded in a rectangular piece of cloth, sixty square inches or so, apparently torn from a bedsheet. Those things were gently removed and placed aside, the detectives taking care to preserve them for closer inspection at a later time. The whole scene, according to the *Buffalo Evening News*, caused even seasoned detectives Cusack and Kennedy "to wince."

Aside from a small white undershirt, the girl's body was completely nude. Advanced stages of decomposition had already set in and positive identification by visual assessment was impossible, but one thing was obvious – considerable violence had been done to the child prior to her being discarded in Swan Lake. At a glance, Dr. Danser later told reporters, she appeared to have been in the water for at least five or six days, perhaps more. Precisely ten days had elapsed from the time Marian was last seen to the time the body in front of them had been found and pulled from the lake.

The head was badly decomposed, but clear evidence remained of a deep laceration to the skull. The *Buffalo Courier*, later covering Dr. Danser's sworn testimony at the inquest, stated: "There was a wound 7/8 of an inch long in the scalp to the bone. It was a ragged wound, as if made with a blunt instrument. The tongue was protruding. The trunk was bottle-green and swollen. The abdomen was partially denuded. There was a mark of the rope on the umbilicus and on other parts of the body." Despite the decomposition a good amount of hair remained, although that, the *Evening News* reported, had been "blackened with muck from the bottom of the creek, but in places it was seen to be light in color."

"Its mouth was in worse shape than any other part of the body," the *Buffalo Express* would write the following morning. "It was swollen to an abnormal size and the police said last night that that swelling had not been caused by the water. Its upper teeth were said to be missing. It was suggested by Dr. Danser that this might be because the gums were badly swelled, but the police don't think so. They suspect that the teeth were knocked out. They also say that it looks very much as if the child had been gagged after it had been assaulted."

The manner in which the poor girl had been tied up was then studied closely. Her body had been bound using two lengths of rope (or clothesline) tied to end-to-end, and together they spanned about twelve feet. From Dr. Danser's later testimony: "In taking the rope off it was found to contain a noose drawn tight about the neck and knotted at the back. Another noose was at the middle, and a third at the ankles."

Additional pieces of twine were also involved, and the *Evening News*, in its coverage, was (perhaps unnecessarily) specific in describing the manner in which the child had been done up: "The whole was tied with rope. One piece of rope tied the legs together at the ankles; another piece was fastened about the middle; a third rope extended from that at the ankles to the rope around the middle; a fourth rope formed a loop extending from the waist about the neck and back to the waist again. This had bitten deeply into the neck and at first sight suggested strangulation. The arms were bound at the sides with a piece of twine. The job was a bungling one."

Next detectives assessed the individual newspapers she'd been wrapped up in, or what was left of them. Slowly and carefully unfolding the portions which hadn't already rotted away and placing them aside to dry, the officers were able to discern that the pages had come from two separate issues of two separate publications: one was the *Evening News*' February 16, 1902 edition, and the other was from the *Courier* of December 16, 1901. These, along with the ropes and piece of cloth the bundle had been wrapped up with, were bagged up as evidence and taken back to the tenth precinct.

As for the vicious assault the poor child had weathered, police surmised this likely had occurred during "somebody's insane freak," as the *Buffalo Evening Times* put it, or "the child might have been accidently killed by a madman, who then attempted to conceal the crime by disposing of the body in the manner it was disposed of." The body clearly had been "violently used," the *Express* wrote, and in describing its condition some publications soon were employing a curious euphemism of the day: her remains, it was said, were found to have been "outraged."

According to Merriam-Webster, contextually relevant definitions of the word "outrage," when used in noun form, include "an act of violence or brutality." As a verb, the word means to "violate the standards or principles of," and in yet another variation it refers directly to the act of rape. It was the closest any of the papers came to stating outright that the girl had been violated in that particular fashion, however by the horrible looks of things nothing of the sort was off the table entirely. Dr. Danser, speaking briefly with the press, refused to get into specifics. "It is too terrible to think of," was his only comment.

So concluded the preliminary examination of the young Jane Doe found floating in the little lake up at Forest Lawn Cemetery. And, the *Express* wrote, "it did not take more than one or two glances from Detective Cornish for him to make up his mind that it was the body of the Murphy child. Detective Palmer looked at it, too, and he said he did not think there was any mistake about it."

It was late on a Friday night, but suddenly there was a mountain of work to be done and sleep wasn't on anyone's itinerary. The top priority right now, everybody all agreed, was carrying the dreadful news to the girl's father, and arranging for him to come in and make a positive identification.

* * * * * *

Cornelius Murphy was at home that Friday night, as it was nearly midnight, and the patrolman who knocked on his door was discreet, for those were his orders. "That policeman was given positive instructions not to breathe a word to Mrs. Murphy about what her husband was wanted for," the *Buffalo Express* explained. "Murphy was cautioned not to tell his wife anything about the finding of the body until it had been identified more positively."

That paper, which apparently had managed to get a reporter down to the morgue ahead of time, best described what happened next:

"When he arrived at the Morgue, Murphy was shown immediately into the room in which his child's body was. He stared at the Morgue officials and the detectives about the body. Then he looked at the little corpse on the slab in front of him. He held his hat in his hand. He had a hard time controlling his feelings and he tugged at his hat, at the same time trying to speak. He could not at first. He scrutinized the little body in front of him from head to foot."

Finally, Cornelius spoke. "That robe settles it," he said, referring to the little white undershirt the girl had on at her discovery, the only thing standing between her and complete nudity.

"Is it your child?" Detective Cornish asked after a moment, in need of something more definitive.

"I guess it is," Cornelius replied sadly. "I guess it's her. I won't swear positively to it, but I think it is. Let me take those things up to my wife. She'll know." He was talking about the clothing the poor thing had been found in, which Dr. Danser initially told him was not an option.

Cornelius asked if he ought to then bring his wife down to the morgue.

"Better not," advised Detective Cornish, who was well aware of Mary Murphy's extremely fragile state of health.

The doctors and the detectives then conferred privately, and after a moment a compromise was reached. Dr. Danser would release the little white undershirt to the detectives, and the detectives would accompany Cornelius to his home and present the garment to his wife for identification. It was then proposed, by someone, that an additional artifact be taken along for the avoidance of all doubt. From the *Buffalo Courier*: "A pathetic incident occurred. It was suggested that if a lock of the hair was washed that might aid in the identification.

The scissors were brought into play and a bit of the hair that once had been golden was clipped from the dead child's head." With that Cornelius was driven home in a fire and accident dispatch wagon, and Detective Cornish followed behind on his bicycle.

The vehicle carrying Cornelius was the first to arrive at 257 West Avenue, but rather than going inside and preparing his wife for the traumatic news incoming he instead chose to remain out front awaiting Detective Cornish, who carried with him the hair and the undershirt found on the little girl back at the morgue. Some reporters arrived ahead of Cornish, and they were somewhat surprised to find Cornelius just sort of lingering there out in front of his house.

"Why don't you go in?" one of them asked.

"I want everyone to go in when I do," was Cornelius's response.

Detective Cornish arrived, as did Detective Palmer, and they were soon joined at the scene by Captain Kilroy.

"Now," announced Cornelius, "I don't want anything said to Mrs. Murphy unless everyone is present."

"Why don't you?" Detective Cornish shot back, now seemingly suspicious of the man's decidedly queer behavior. "What's the matter?"

"Oh, er, I want everything open and above-board," Cornelius stammered. "That's all."

The three officers then walked up the little hill leading to the Murphy home, Cornelius trailing closely behind. "Come along, boys," Kilroy called out to the press as he approached the front door and rang the bell.

After a moment Mary Murphy appeared at the door. She'd been asleep on the sofa in the sitting room, where she had spent the last ten sleepless, hazy and torturous nights. "It is here that she has slept every night since the child left home," the *Express* duly noted, "hoping that some news would be received during the night of the little one's whereabouts, and that she could be right at the door to answer the messenger's ring."

Mary was asked to go upstairs and get dressed, and while they waited the detectives and the newsmen made themselves at home there in the sitting room. Cornelius waited there with them, and – to the *Express* reporter, at least – a newly-existing tension seemed to be developing between the dead girl's father and the senior investigator on the case.

The two eyed each other uncomfortably, and as they did Detective Cornish withdrew from his pocket the little undershirt, slowly unfolding it from the paper he'd wrapped it up in. "Don't show her that," sniped Cornelius. "Ask her some questions first. Don't show her that first."

As this was happening Mary Murphy descended the front steps, entering the room from the front hall and bracing herself for the absolute worst.

"Is she dead?" she put forth plaintively.

"Come with me," replied Captain Kilroy, leading her through the dining room and into the kitchen. One by one the detectives entered into the small room as well, but when Cornelius tried to follow he was halted by Kilroy, who abruptly held up his hand, traffic cop-style.

"Just let us talk to her alone," the captain said. "You wait in here for awhile." Reluctantly Cornelius complied, taking a seat and speaking instead with the group of newsmen on hand, each of them eager to hear and write down every last word he had to say.

While he was doing this the two detectives from headquarters arrived – Chief of Detectives Patrick Cusack and Detective Sergeant

Hugh Kennedy – and right away they were shown into the kitchen. Cornelius and the reporters watched as another party then descended the stairs carrying the undershirt, joining the group in the kitchen and, presumably, presenting the sad garment to the missing girl's mother. Everyone hushed up and listened from the outside. Then, through the door, Mary Murphy's voice could be discerned.

"That's it," she was heard to say. "That's hers."

Cornelius again applied for entry into the room, but once again he was denied by Captain Kilroy. Then the door opened and his wife appeared, steadying herself as she stepped out and crossed the sitting room, barely making her way over to a large armchair before collapsing altogether from the shock and the grief. She "seemed about to faint," the *Express* reported, so "she was given a stimulant" in order that she might retain some measure of composure. "Opiates were administered to quiet her," the *Courier* weighed in. "It is said that she is in a very bad condition."

Either way, Mary did come to and remain alert long enough to present the papers with the following statement:

"Her little soul's in heaven. That's her body all right. The shirt is hers. There's no doubt of it. She's dead and God's will be done. It seems strange she should have been taken off like that. If she had only been taken sick and died, or even if she's been killed by a street car – anything but this terrible thing. The suspense; oh, it's terrible."

FIVE

Formalities

It was past midnight, now into the very earliest hours of Saturday, June 28.

Their business at the Murphy home concluded, the men of the tenth precinct now returned to their Niagara Street stationhouse, Captain Kilroy asking Cornelius to come along to complete a more formal interview. They were met there by Chief Cusack and Detective Kennedy, and everyone convened in the captain's private office.

Inside, the *Buffalo Courier* wrote, Cornelius was "plied with questions calculated to bring out any further facts of which he might be in possession and which were calculated to shed light upon the mysterious and revolting crime. The questions were pointed and rapid, and as seen through the glass door, some of them put to the taste of a man undergoing interrogation. Indeed, the proceeding savored very much of the 'sweat-box' inquisition. At the end of half an hour he was allowed to depart and the officers remained within to hold a conference on such new facts, if any, they had brought to light by their interrogating."

While Kilroy, Cusack and Kennedy were all busy strategizing behind closed doors, Detectives Cornish and Palmer had gone back over to the Murphy residence to perform what the *Courier* called a "quiet search," gently looking about for any items that may be relevant to their investigation. In particular, they were looking for any old newspapers - especially those bearing dates proximal to the ones found wrapped around Marian's body - and also for any rope or clothesline similar to that which had been used to bundle her up.

It was about 1:15 a.m. when Cornelius stepped out of the stationhouse, declaring to the group of reporters there that he was going back to the morgue to make arrangements for the burial of his child. They all watched as he then walked off alone down Niagara Street.

Despite the late hour, officials were still at the morgue when Cornelius arrived there around 1:40 a.m. Before he could claim his daughter's body, however, he was told an official autopsy needed to be conducted. "Morgue officials informed him they were not yet ready to turn the remains of the child over to the family," wrote the *Courier*, "and that there would be plenty of time in which to make arrangements for the funeral. Murphy was mildly regretful at this announcement, but did not make any particular objections to the delay."

He was, however, allowed a second viewing of his child. In the company of Dr. Danser and a Sergeant McDonald, Cornelius spent ten solemn minutes sitting with the girl's remains, and his observations during that time only solidified his certainty that the body was that of his daughter. "His wife had told him to examine a vaccination mark and also look for a bruise about the third fingernail of the left hand," the *Courier* explained. "He had found both marks and was satisfied of the identification beyond doubt."

Before he could depart Cornelius was set upon by reporters, and despite the late hour and the gravity of the moment he took the time to field their torrent of questions, giving terse and guarded answers as to what he did and did not know concerning his daughter's terrible demise.

The *Buffalo Express*, when issued later that morning, would carry the following lengthy interview, conducted as Cornelius was preparing to exit the morgue:

"Do you suspect anyone?" Murphy was asked.

"Whom would you suspect?" he replied. Then he said: "When I walked in just now and saw them pull out the thing on which my little girl lay, I thought it was my child lying asleep. But, of course, when I came to look at the face the lines were gone. Yet I knew it was my little girl."

"What is the name of the person you suspect?" asked a reporter from the Express.

"I'm not saying anything," answered Murphy, "because until tonight I would not believe that any human being would be monster enough to do such a thing."

"Was your child assaulted?"

"No," said Murphy.

"How do you know?"

"Well, I don't think she was. At least, I have not been told she was."

"How long do you believe the body has been in the water?"

"I have no way of knowing that, have I?" said Murphy.

"It was in longer than a day, was it not?"

"I can't tell how long it was in."

"You think she was not thrown in the water the first night after being kidnaped?"

"She never went near the water of her own account, anyhow," replied the father.

"Where do you think the clothes are?" asked The Express man.

"Why, they would burn them, wouldn't they?"

"What makes you think that?"

"So there would not be any trace of her left, and the police would not know."

"What was there around the body?"

"There were newspapers and the little shirt she had on; the other clothes were not there."

"Do you think the police will ever find those?"

"I don't think they ever will."

"Do you think there was more than one person in this affair?" said the reporter.

"Why?" asked Murphy.

"Because you said 'they' burned the clothes."

"How could one person have got her over the fence alone?" said the father.

"What fence?"

"Forest Lawn."

"Why should they have to put her over the fence?"

"Because," said Murphy, "the gates of Forest Lawn close at 6 o'clock."

"How do you know?"

"Someone told me."

"Who was it?"

"I don't remember."

"What part of the fence did they put her over?"

"I don't know that; how should I know it?" said Murphy.

"Then you believe they put her over the fence and dropped her into the water where she was found?"

"I didn't say that, except as I know she would never go near the water of her own accord."

"Then they took her there after 6 o'clock at night, you think?"

"They must have."

"You think that was the night she was kidnaped?"

"I am sure I don't know about that."

"If it wasn't that night where do you think they kept her until they did throw her in?"

"I don't know; and come to think of it, I believe they got her that night after she left home, tied her up, took her out there, hoisted her over the fence and threw her in."

"Well, Mr. Murphy, you say they did not assault her, so why should they have taken her off the street, burned her clothes, left nothing but a shirt on her, wrapped her in newspapers, tied ropes around her, taken her out there, hoisted her over the fence, and thrown her in?"

"Well, do you think they could have kept her for ransom, and then, when they found out such a muss was being made about it, sneaked out there some night and thrown her in?"

"Then you are quite sure there was more than one in it?"

"Yes, because how could only one have hoisted her over the fence?"

"Are you very sure she was hoisted over the fence?"

"Well, I believe they took her out there, hoisted her over the fence, and threw her in."

"Have the police any clue?"

"I don't want to talk about what the police are doing."

"They talked with you at police station No. 10, didn't they?"

"Why, yes. Naturally, I wouldn't say anything what they talked to me about."

"Did anything they said to you point to any definite clue or toward suspecting anyone?"

"No, not that I know of, because all that I know is that I never knew until I saw that little body that anyone could do such a thing. I didn't think there was anyone alive who could do it."

At 4 a.m., just ahead of first light, a detail of policemen from the sixth precinct headed back up to Forest Lawn Cemetery to perform an end-to-end search of the grounds, hoping to find the remainder of Marian's missing clothes or anything else that may point them in the direction of the killer.

It was just past 9 a.m. when Superintendent Bull arrived at headquarters, officially taking direct charge over the investigation and naming Chief Cusack his active lieutenant on the case. On Bull's orders, the *Courier* reported, "no time or money at his disposal shall be spared in running down the murderer who has added the atrocious crime to Buffalo's history." And, before going into a private conference with Cusack, Bull made clear that his office would not be engaging in wanton acts of speculation for the benefit of the press. "I have no theories," he gruffly proclaimed to a *Buffalo Evening News* reporter. "What we want is facts."

It was around noon when, once again, Cornelius came calling at the morgue, this time in the company of two close family members. One was his brother, Michael J. Murphy, who resided there in Buffalo and was still holding out hope that the body of the girl lying dead inside was not that his of niece. The other was his brother-in-law, Mary's brother, John O'Brien. The three men were shown inside, and according to the *Courier* when they exited several minutes later each of the girl's uncles were weeping openly. Cornelius, on the other hand, had "gazed at his child without a tremor" and "remained as stolid as before."

"With no outward sign of emotion at the horrible sight," the *Courier* wrote, Cornelius then "walked from the chapel of the morgue to the reception room. There without a tremor he picked up the three morning papers and read them carefully. After he had finished one he picked up the other and read all that had been printed about him and his family." After making his way through the last of it, Cornelius folded up the newspapers and put them off to one side. As he did, he was heard to say: "I have been terribly misquoted."

Josephine Mumm, the family's domestic, was called into the tenth precinct a little later that day, with Captain Kilroy taking her statement in the presence of Chief Cusack, Detective Cornish and a few others. There she fielded "a cross-fire of questions," as the *Courier* put it, the desk sergeant transcribing her answers and filling three full pages before having a patrolman drive her back to her place of work on West Avenue.

The Murphy household, by this point, was now officially in mourning and closed to visitors, a heavy chain drawn across the front door to ward off any unknown callers or unwanted solicitors. Reporters who came knocking were summarily turned away, and those who did gain access to Cornelius found him suddenly "taciturn" and none too willing to speak with the papers. As for his wife, the *Courier* reported that Mary looked to be devastated completely, appearing "worn and haggard" and remaining essentially bedridden.

If Cornelius seemed abruptly hostile and standoffish toward members of the local press, it was likely due to their jarring treatment of him in the rash of coverage since his daughter's heartbreaking discovery. The *Buffalo Evening Times*, when published that evening, was the first to break that salacious bit of gossip concerning Cornelius's previous confinements to the local asylum, and now the streets were abuzz with rumor and speculation. For instance, the *Evening Times* wrote: "There was a report all over town this afternoon to the effect that Cornelius Murphy had been arrested. [Michael] Murphy, who was seen at the Murphy home this afternoon, stated that he has heard the report through the children."

Mary's brother John O'Brien, a decorator by trade, was unmarried and had lived periodically with the Murphy family, and as such he was fairly quick to come to the patriarch's defense. "It's not right to suspect Murphy of the murder of his child," he told a *Courier* reporter later that afternoon. "What right have the police to think he did it? Do I think he did it? Why, no, of course I don't. I don't think he'd do anything like that."

In fact, another (unnamed) relative suggested to the *Evening Times*: "He ought to sue the papers."

* * * * * *

Cornelius rose early the following morning, a damp and gloomy Sunday, June 29.

Along with his brother-in-law John O'Brien and his servant girl Josephine Mumm, he left his home by carriage shortly after 7 a.m., collected by Detective Cornish and another patrolman and escorted to the morgue for one last look at his little girl in advance of the autopsy later that morning. Josephine, the *Buffalo Courier* wrote, "was there for the purpose of aiding in the identification" of the body beyond the last whisper of a doubt, as she was the one "who had always attended the child, washing and dressing it."

As such it took the girl very little time to provide her affirmation, and with that Marian's body was wheeled into a back room for the commencement of the official post-mortem examination. Anxious to learn the results, Cornelius and his entourage passed the time by making their way up to Allentown to attend the 10 a.m. mass at Immaculate Conception Church, and after heading home for a brief nap he paid a visit to undertaker Thomas F. Crowley at 145 Franklin Street, making arrangements for his daughter's funeral to take place the following day.

The autopsy of Marian Murphy had been scheduled for 9 a.m., but it was late in getting underway due to Erie County Medical Examiner Earl Danser's delayed arrival. Just about everyone involved, at this point, seemed less than thrilled with Dr. Danser's lack of professional enthusiasm, with the *Courier* remarking on his "diliatoriness" and the *Buffalo Evening News* criticizing his "leisurely methods." When finally he did arrive – unkempt, unshaven and seemingly without much sleep – Danser and Deputy Medical Examiner John Howland were met by First Assistant District Attorney Frederick A. Haller, whose "duty was purely legal," the *Courier* reported, "his purpose being to be a witness to the examination and to see that the autopsy was performed according to the law."

The doctors began their work around 9:40 a.m., methodically reviewing every inch of the child's corpse from head to toe. A weight of fifty pounds was recorded, although the *Buffalo Evening Times* noted that "the child is said to have weighed only 35 pounds" in life, the extra taken on during her time spent submerged underwater. Her brain, for its part, weighed in at forty-five ounces and was noted as being in a moderate state of decomposition.

The scalp had been partially denuded of hair, and a head wound measuring seven-eighths of an inch in length was indicated. Not severe enough to be fatal, the cut nonetheless would have been more than sufficient to stun or otherwise incapacitate a small child. "It was a ragged wound and did not look as if it was done by a sharp instrument," Danser would later testify. "A blunt instrument must have produced it."

There were, he added, two visible contusions on the girl's head and another on her forehead, "the eyes were bulging and bruised" and "the tongue was protruding through the teeth." Each of Marian's top two front teeth had been knocked out by force, and from the back of her throat the doctors retrieved a piece of masticated chewing gum, something she was known to have purchased on the night of her disappearance.

Her stomach was found to contain four ounces of partially-digested food, and a preliminary analysis of that food suggested it to be meat and potatoes – a meal in keeping with the one Josephine had fed her right before she'd gone out and gone missing. Between the stomach contents and the chewing gum, the medical professionals surmised that Marian's life had quite likely been extinguished a short while after she had consumed those things.

Each of the lungs were collapsed and showed symptoms of congestion, and when placed in water they both floated at the surface. This was taken as an indication that the girl's death could not have been caused by drowning, as their buoyancy proved there was no water inside weighing them down. "In my opinion Marian Murphy came to her death by asphyxiation," Danser would later testify, "caused by strangling," likely "from the cord around the neck." He could not, however, entirely rule out suffocation.

The worst of it came last. The uterus was examined and found to be normal, however the vagina was dilated and it showed numerous lacerations. A nearly-inch-long gash had been made upon the child's vulva, and another roughly half that length extended back through the perineum. Both the hymen and the fourchette had been destroyed. It was almost unthinkable, but the not-quite-six-year-old girl lying on the table before them had suffered a savage and brutal sex assault prior to – or possibly immediately after – her killing.

The proceedings drew to a close around 1 p.m., nearly three and a half hours after they had begun. Frederick Haller, the assistant district attorney, was the first to exit the operating room, and to the waiting members of the press he declined to issue a comment, having advised the medical examiners each to do the same. Dr. Danser emerged a short while later, the *Evening News* reported, and when asked about his findings he simply "regarded the clouds and seemed inclined to think that some other day would do as well." As he shuffled off he called back that his office was very busy, but he would share the results of the autopsy once they had been formally committed to paper.

Returning to his office three hours later Dr. Danser was again approached by reporters, and this time they were able to get a bit more out of him. After a fair amount of cajoling he allowed that the manner of death, in his opinion, had been asphyxiation and not drowning – "that is," he told the *Courier*, "she had been choked to death." And while he did allow that she had been criminally assaulted, he failed to mention that a prominent aspect of that attack been sexual in nature, instead referencing only "certain lacerations" found upon her body.

When asked how long he believed Marian's body had been concealed in Swan Lake, Danser said that "it would be difficult to tell the exact time, but the decomposition had reached a stage indicating that the remains had been in the water from seven to ten days. I think perhaps a little longer than seven, but not longer than ten." Further examination, he added, would be done under a microscope, and a chemist by the name of Dr. John A. Miller had been brought in to more closely analyze various organs, as well as the rope used to bind and most likely strangle the young child.

Back at the Murphy home preparations were being made for Marian's funeral, and a *Courier* reporter who swung by that afternoon was witness to an especially heartbreaking exchange between the girl's mother and her slightly-older sibling. From the following morning's edition:

Angela, the 8 year old sister, scarcely knows what has become of her sister. Several days ago the bright-eyed youngster after hearing her parents discussing the kidnaping theory, nestled in her mother's lap and said: "Mamma, they didn't kidnap my little sister, did they? I want to see Marian. I want you to get her and bring her back. I haven't any little playmate now."

The child, who scarcely knows what death is, does not realize yet that Marian will not be brought back to her. She knows vaguely that something terrible has happened, but she has not been told what it is.

Yesterday Angela was asking for Marian. "When are they going to bring Marian home? It seems so funny around the house without her; I haven't anyone to play with now. Mamma, did my auntie take Marian to her home?" was her pathetic cry.

It is hard for a mother to lose a child as Mrs. Murphy has lost Marian, but how doubly hard it must be to have to evade the innocent questions of the dead one's sister.

At the tenth precinct, meanwhile, a fresh clue had turned up and a renewed flourish of activity was underway. William H. Baker was an attorney with Bartlett, Baker & Horton, a law firm on the sixth floor of the Prudential Building downtown, and all the stepped-up newspaper coverage had prompted him to recall an incident that had transpired back on June 17, the night of Marian's disappearance. That evening, Baker told police, his nearly-seven-year-old daughter Madeline had left their home at 341 Jersey Street to visit the grocery store, and she'd come running back after an unsettling encounter with a stranger a few streets over.

While walking up Porter Avenue, about a half a block west of Holy Angels Church, Madeline and two other little girls were approached by what the *Courier* called a "young negro," a man with a friendly demeanor and a tidy appearance. He was dressed in a gray suit and wearing a light fedora, and Madeline was certain she had seen him around the area before, approaching and talking with other neighborhood girls roughly her age.

"Hello, little girl!" the man had exclaimed, addressing Madeline directly. "Would you like to go with me to get some ice cream and cake?"

"No," she'd politely demurred, her intuition telling her to back away and to keep it moving.

"Come on down to the band concert with me," the man persisted, referring to the outdoor bandstand at the Front, reiterating his promise to buy her some sweets if she did.

With that the girl had broken into a scared sprint, dashing home to tell her mother and father all about the uncomfortable exchange. He hadn't though too much of it at the time, Baker told the officers, but in light of all that had transpired since he now believed that this gentleman may have gone on to abduct the Murphy girl a little later that evening, and that his daughter Madeline might be in a position to identify the man if he were put before her.

The lead was assigned to Detective George Palmer, and Palmer headed over to the Baker residence to meet with the attorney and his daughter. Together the three of them retraced the steps the girl had taken that evening, with Madeline pinpointing the house at 410 Porter as the one in front of which she had been approached.

The *Courier*, meanwhile, rather provocatively pointed out that Baker's account "established beyond all doubt the story that a negro had been prowling in and about the streets adjacent to the Murphy home on the very night that Marian Murphy was kidnaped."

In fact, that paper wrote the following morning: "On the basis of this story it was intimated at No. 10 Station last night that several suspicious negroes might be taken in custody today to be scrutinized by the child."

* * * * * *

The funeral for Marian Murphy was held the following day, Monday, June 30.

At 10 a.m. undertaker Thomas Crowley departed the morgue with the girl's body in tow, transporting it by carriage to the Murphy family's West Avenue home, where a reception was scheduled to take place throughout the afternoon. A crowd had already assembled there when he arrived a short while later, everybody watching as her tiny casket was carried up the front steps and into the house. A funeral crepe was hung from the door.

For the next several hours Marian's body lie resting in the dining room, the most spacious one in the small house, her little coffin outlined in white plush with a silver engraved inscription plate reading, simply, "Our Darling." The condition of her body, naturally, rendered the viewing a closed-casket affair. "Many people called at the home during the few hours the body rested there," the *Buffalo Express* reported, and "almost every person in the neighborhood sent some kind of an offering to the little one who had been so cruelly murdered. Little girls and boys brought flowers in their arms and asked to be allowed to lay them on the casket."

Aside from his brother Michael, who lived right there in Buffalo,

Cornelius had three other siblings residing elsewhere in the state, and they had come pouring into town to pay their respects and to attend the funeral services. Hugh Murphy lived in Fulton, a freshly-incorporated city to the northwest of Syracuse, as did his sister, whom the papers identified as Mrs. M.F. Crahan. They were joined by another sister, a Mrs. Arthur Spaulding of Syracuse, as well as Mary Murphy's only sister, Mrs. Charles Orcutt of Syracuse.

Mary, for her part, was not holding up well. It had been expected that she would accompany the cortege to the church for the funeral service, but the *Buffalo Evening News* reported that by that point she was in such "pitiful condition" that she'd been forced to remain at home. From the following morning's *Express*: "It was intended that Mrs. Murphy should attend the funeral of her little daughter if she possibly could, but when the casket was moved from the house she swooned and drugs had to be used to restore her."

The funeral procession consisted of five horse-drawn carriages, and at around 2:30 p.m. it began winding its way over to Immaculate Conception Church, located on Edward Street at the southwest corner of Morgan Avenue (today called South Elmwood Avenue). The huge, sandstone Catholic cathedral had been expanded two years previously, but according to the *Evening News* it had reached near-capacity before the mourners had even departed West Avenue (the church still stands, although it would fall into considerable disrepair over the years and close its doors in 2005; today it is the home of Assembly House 150, an architectural workshop and studio space focused on nurturing excellence in that field).

The official services were conducted by Reverend Thomas Donohue, the parish rector, along with his assistant, Reverend Edward McShane. Inside, the *Express* noted, "almost every woman in the congregation wept as the casket was moved slowly up the aisle." The pallbearers were four of Marian's little playmates – James Helsdon, Oxley Goshorn, Keith McDougall and Russell Carrick. Cornelius was next in the procession, followed by his brothers and sisters. "When the casket reached the altar six candles were placed upon it," the *Express* wrote, the Reverends Donohue and McShane then conducting the funeral mass, commemorating the child's untimely passing in accordance with the prescribed rites of the Roman Catholic Church.

Following that the procession headed out of the city, travelling along South Park Avenue and eventually reaching Ridge Road in what is now the city of Lackawanna. Back in 1902 the area was still called Limestone Hill, a part of West Seneca, and the mourning carriages were bound for Holy Cross Cemetery, a 191-acre burial site to the southeast of that intersection. The final resting place of many an early Irish immigrant, Holy Cross Cemetery (formerly Limestone Hill Cemetery) was then a vast and placid burial ground, not yet overshadowed by the enormous and world-renown Our Lady of Victory Basilica, which would come to define that corner upon its construction in the 1920s.

According to cemetery records, Marian was interred in division four, one of its oldest and earliest-developed portions, just west of the Garden of Coronation. A worn and faded ledger indicates her final resting spot is located in row I, grave number 49, although many of the markers from this time have deteriorated badly and are well beyond all hope of recognition.

* * * * * *

If one good thing managed to come about that day it did so in the form of a statement from the Buffalo Police Department, clearing Cornelius of any and all suspicion in his daughter's slaying. "The developments of the autopsy are considered to have vindicated the innocence of the unhappy father, Cornelius V. Murphy," the *Buffalo Evening News* would report later that evening. "It was not the intention of the police to accuse him. They merely questioned him as a matter of form and because there was nothing else to do, thanks to the leisurely methods of the County Medical Examiners, who could see no reason for hurry in such a case. But the fact that he was questioned secretly led to rumors that he was under suspicion."

A *Buffalo Courier* reporter had obtained a lengthy comment from one police official, whom the paper identified only by stating that he "is one of the detectives who has been at work on the case since the finding of little Marian's body, and he is credited with being one of the best and most thorough men connected with the Detective Bureau." The notion of Cornelius being the guilty party, he said, was without so much as a shred of supporting evidence, and the misperception likely stemmed from the interview the bereaved father had granted the *Buffalo Express* prior to leaving the morgue early Saturday morning.

"Suspicion has been cast upon a certain person since the night the child's body was found, but I will tell you frankly, that I have not suspected him of the crime at any time," the detective said, speaking of Cornelius. "Of course, I know that a great many people about the city seem to be of the opinion that the person was responsible for the little girl's death, and I believe that idea was largely formed by an interview printed in one of the morning papers, in which that person was placed on the rack by a reporter and asked questions of such a nature that when the interview was read the natural assumption would be that the person was under suspicion. I have worked pretty hard on this case and looked up each point carefully, and can't see, for the life of me, where there is any room to suspect the person everyone believes we have our eyes on. He is just as innocent as I am, and it is wrong for anyone to believe him guilty of this until we had facts to warrant it. So far we have absolutely nothing, at least not against that person."

And while Buffalo's finest had thus far been unable to make any headway in determining the killer's actual identity, the *Courier* now assured its readers that there was a ray of hope on the horizon. In that morning's coverage the paper had boasted that "two of the leading detective agencies of the country are anxious to send several of their best detectives here for the purpose of working on the Marian Murphy case," and that "these agencies, one of which already has a representative here, are only awaiting the announcement of a good-sized reward, when they will put their men on the case."

The matter of a reward offering, actually, had been raised at the previous week's meeting of the city's Board of Aldermen (Buffalo, up until 1915, relied on a system of "city fathers," elected from various wards, to govern its affairs). At that time Alderman Louis Mullenhoff had introduced a resolution that would see the city offer a $1,000 reward for information leading to the capture and conviction of the guilty party. That motion was to be addressed in today's meeting, and there had been speculation that the amount would balloon to as much as $10,000 in light of all the nationwide news exposure.

When the Board of Aldermen did convene that afternoon, however, the highly-contentious session failed to yield the expected increase, with some board members arguing against a financial incentive altogether. When the dust settled it was decided that, pending the mayor's approval, a reward in the amount of $1,000 would be offered up in the Marian Murphy case, with an additional $1,000 being allocated for information pertaining to a more-recent crime that was presently grabbing headlines right alongside it – two nights earlier, on June 28, four men had walked into a First Ward saloon and executed its proprietor, 37-year-old Austin Crowe, then fleeing the Fulton Street establishment and managing to evade capture thus far.

With regards to the efforts of local authorities, the *Evening News* reported that "a general negro hunt" was presently underway throughout the city, this owing to the tip provided by attorney William Baker concerning the unknown black male who had approached his daughter Madeline on the night of Marian's vanishing. "Wherever a black man is seen who appears in any degree suspicious, he is questioned," the paper explained, "and unless he can give a good account of himself the order is to arrest him."

One such interaction had taken place earlier that morning, a tenth precinct patrolman named Michael Conley noticing a young black gentleman acting suspiciously down at the foot of Porter Avenue. He'd been prowling about a women's shelter house there, and at Conley's approach the man had taken off running, halting only when the officer drew his gun and threatened to shoot. He was arrested on suspicion of being a tramp, then hauled back to the station to account for his whereabouts on the night of June 17.

There the man gave his name as James Wright, and his age as twenty-two. He refused to say, however, how long he had been in Buffalo or where he'd come from previously. William and Madeline Baker were sent for, in the hopes that the young girl would be able to identify Wright as the fellow who'd tried luring her off to the Front, but upon viewing him Madeline stated definitively that he was not the one she'd seen on Porter Avenue that night. That man, the girl told police, had worn nicer clothes.

Another black man was picked up later that night, seen hopping from a moving train as it passed along the foot of Hudson Street by patrolman Alois Wohirab of the tenth precinct. "At the station the prisoner described himself as Thomas Seavey, a Kansan, 23 years old," the *Express* wrote. "He said he had come from Pittsburg on the train from which he had jumped. An investigation proved that the train had come from Pittsburg and Captain Kilroy locked Seavey up as a tramp."

Neither of the two men had had any involvement, but with the Baker clue being their only functioning lead police were hardly ready to stop shaking down questionable-looking colored men in the area. Madeline's father was especially keen on running down the man who had spoken with his daughter, so incensed was he at the thought of such a fiend preying on innocent little children of the neighborhood.

"I am going to try to find this negro and if I do I intend to make him suffer," the attorney told the *Buffalo Evening Times*, "whether he is the one who murdered the Murphy child or not. I think any father is justified in shooting a negro who would accost his child and offer to buy it candy. I think I can locate several persons who saw the negro speak to my child and if this is true we shall be able to take him into custody and then set at rest whether or not there is any truth in the negro theory."

SIX

Zeroing In

As things stood, the *Buffalo Evening News* wrote the following day, July 1, police were "as far from the arrest of the fiend who committed the crimes as they were two weeks ago tomorrow morning."

That evening would mark the two-week anniversary of the bizarre and frightening disappearance of Marian Murphy, and the city's populace was quickly losing faith in the ability of its local police force to solve the crime, or even to serve and protect in the most basic manner.

Across the city worried citizens were voicing their concerns, and the *Buffalo Evening Times* reported that it had received a number of letters from panicky parents pointing to a growing hysteria: "In some letters it was stated that in Buffalo mothers were in fear to remain home alone at night; children were in danger from kidnappers and worse, if they went on the street while fathers hardly dared to go out at night for fear of being waylaid by foot-pads and murderers."

Many of those complaints, the *Evening Times* wrote, included a "bitter denunciation" of Police Superintendent William Bull, whose leadership already had fallen into question; it was widely known, for instance, that he had clashed with his second-in-command, Chief of Detectives Patrick Cusack, who had attempted to advance the drowning theory back while Bull was still married to the kidnapping angle. This, in conjunction with a slew of other failures yet to come, would eventually lead to Bull's being relieved of his position in 1906.

Mostly, though, the papers blamed the lack of progress not on the individual officers and detectives but instead on the city's mayor, Erastus C. Knight, who had implemented a curious system of rotating men from one district to another every four months. From the *Evening Times*: "The difficulty with the police does not seem to lie so much in the men themselves as it does in the rotten system in vogue – the shifting of men from districts in which they are familiar with every alley way and hiding place and know every crook in the vicinity."

It was Chief Cusack, then, who stepped up as top man in the investigation, establishing a makeshift office for himself at the tenth precinct over on Niagara Street. With him he'd brought four headquarters detectives – Jim Sullivan, Jerry Lynch, John Devine and Louis Henafelt – and that station's captain, Patrick Kilroy, was now at Cusack's disposal. Between the two of them press conferences were organized multiple times a day, with detectives working around the clock and with next to no sleep.

The county also was gearing up for whatever case it had coming its way, and to that end both Mary Murphy and Josephine Mumm were summoned downtown to the district attorney's office to provide their sworn statements. Erie County's district attorney, in 1902, was Thomas Penney, appointed to that office three years earlier by then-governor of New York Theodore Roosevelt. Multiple witnesses were to be called in for an interview, DA Penney told the *Evening News*, as county authorities would be collaborating with local police to help assemble a profile of the murdered child's killer.

That morning, a Tuesday, Mary and Josephine were picked up at the Murphy home and escorted via closed carriage to the County and City Hall building downtown. At the northwest corner of Franklin and Church Streets, the historic 1870s Victorian Romanesque still stands and remains in function as Old County Hall (Buffalo's City Hall presently occupies its own quarters in nearby Niagara Square). "Mrs. Murphy was dressed in deep black," the *Evening News* noted, adding that "she walked very feebly and had to be assisted" inside the building; Josephine, meanwhile, appeared "radiant in a purple waist and an all-eclipsing hat."

At around that same time, back at the tenth precinct stationhouse, Sergeant George Ward was fielding an incoming tip, and it was yet another account of some suspicious activity in the neighborhood on the night of Marian's taking. Twenty-three-year-old Arthur Goatseay lived with his family on Elm Street, and he and his father Joseph worked together delivering milk on the city's west side. Their shift began before daybreak, and Arthur now claimed to have witnessed something fairly peculiar in the earliest hours of June 18.

While making deliveries along Hudson Street, the younger Goatseay stated, something unusual had caught his eye as he'd made his way past a small house that functioned as a "Chinese laundry." Chinese laundries were common in the early twentieth century, with impoverished immigrants from the Orient finding they could manage a decent living providing this essential neighborhood service, and the one operating at 285 Hudson had come to the milkman's attention as he'd strolled by it at around 4 a.m.

Out of a side door, he told Sergeant Ward, he'd seen a Chinese gentleman emerge wearing what he would later describe to the *Buffalo Courier* as a "long white robe that looked like a night shirt." In his arms the man had been a cradling what "looked like an ordinary bundle of laundry," and after glancing shiftily in each direction he'd made a bee-line for the curb, depositing the parcel in the ash can there before heading straight back inside the house.

"It struck me as being funny at the time," Goatseay told the *Courier*, "but I didn't pay very much attention to it. Then I read of the kidnaping of Marian Murphy, and I began to think perhaps the Chinaman might have had something to do with it. But I did not want to go too fast. I kept thinking over the matter and when I finally read that the little girl had been criminally assaulted, I remembered a Chinaman around the corner had been arrested on that charge once, so I made up my mind to tell the police what I had seen."

Goatseay stated that he now believed the discarded bundle to have contained the clothing of the missing little child, and upon hearing this Sergeant Ward erupted in outright laughter, assuring him that "a Chinaman never did that job." Ward did however pass the details along to Chief Cusack, the *Courier* wrote, and Cusack, by contrast, "believed the information to be of the utmost importance, and acted upon it immediately."

Rather than assigning it to one of his men, the *Courier* noted, Cusack decided to follow up on the tip himself, leaving the station on foot and walking over to the Hudson Street laundry to have a preliminary look around the outside of the premises. Its proximity to the Murphy residence, he felt, in conjunction with the curious and notoriously-secretive habits of the city's Chinese population, most certainly made the spot worthy of a closer look.

The laundry at 285 Hudson Street, actually, had already been entered and searched a week earlier on June 24, not by police detectives but by *Buffalo Evening Times* reporter John Bowen, whose overzealous snooping had brought him to that establishment and seen him waltz right in and begin questioning its proprietor. And, the *Evening Times* reported, Bowen just so happened to come calling on Cusack a short while after the chief had gotten back from checking the place out for himself. On the occasion of his inspection, Bowen told Cusack, he had come across little more than a cache of refuse and old newspapers, however at that time Marian's body had yet to be discovered wrapped in that material, so its presence hadn't sent up any red flags.

After a brief conference between Cusack and three of his detectives – Jim Sullivan, Jerry Lynch and John Devine – the decision was made to return and execute a formal search of the premises. It was shortly after 2:30 p.m. when the four of them set off for Hudson Street, leaving the station with newspaperman Bowen and two other reporters tagging along to witness the raid in real time.

* * * * * *

The wood-frame house at 285 Hudson Street was small and rickety, just one and a half stories tall, consisting of a main floor, an attic and a cellar. Described by the *Buffalo Review* as "somewhat run down," it sat ten or twelve feet back from the sidewalk and gave the impression of being fairly neglected, it's back yard a tangled-up mess of debris and overgrown weeds (the 2,600-square-foot property sits vacant today, although the late-nineteenth century residential cottages on either side remain standing).

In front of the house a red, hand-painted sign read, "Charley We," and underneath it, "Laundry." Charley We was the establishment's proprietor, a Chinese immigrant who had been living and working out of the home for a number of years, and in that time he had become something of a fixture in the neighborhood. *Buffalo Evening Times* reporter John Bowen had learned the previous week that the local kids often gathered to play right out front of We's place, and that Cornelius Murphy himself would occasionally send his clothing there to be restored.

It was about 3 p.m. when Detectives Cusack, Sullivan, Lynch and Devine reached the house, having encountered and collected two additional men – the tenth precinct's Detective Malcolm Cornish and Patrolman John Coughlin – along the way. Now six-strong, the *Buffalo Courier* noted, the raiding party was able to close in on the home with officers approaching from each direction: "Cornish and Coughlin took a position at Hudson Street, at the corner of Plymouth, and Mr. Cusack, with the other three, stood at Hudson Street, at the corner of West Avenue. With the laundry on the south side of the street in the block between them the two forces moved together. They met in front of the house, Cusack stepping forward and entering."

Inside the men found Charley We, sitting behind a counter in his laundry's main office area. He leapt to his feet when Cusack produced his badge, the *Review* wrote, "his eyes rolling with fright and perturbation written in every line of his face." Then, according to the *Buffalo Evening News*, a "look of Mongolian cunning crept into the Mongolian's eyes" as he addressed the officers.

"Two Chilee up 'taire," We declared. "Come flom Canada last night" (the papers, in this case the *Evening News*, seem to have taken great delight back then in mockingly reprinting, more or less verbatim, the broken English of the foreigners they quoted).

This was a just ruse, the *Evening Times* explained, "a pretense that the police were looking for smuggled Chinks," possibly a distraction designed to draw the officers upstairs so We could make his escape. Cusack dispatched a pair of detectives to check the upper level, but after having a quick look around those men came back down and announced that We had effectively, as the saying went, gone pee-pee in their Coke.

All the commotion did however draw out the house's other occupant, another Chinese immigrant named Charley Sing. Sing was only visiting, and he had his own laundry just a couple blocks away at 281 Virginia Street. He was wearing traditional Chinese attire – "dressed up," the *Evening Times* noted, "as on holiday occasions" – and upon finding him there the officers advised both men that they were being detained while detectives had a look around.

The inside of the house, according to the *Review*, was laid out fairly simply. The front hallway opened up into one large room, which was divided in two by a set of board partitions. The front half served as the laundry's main office, while the space behind the divider served as We's makeshift sleeping quarters. The room beyond that was the one containing the wash tubs, where clothes were laundered and subsequently hung to dry, and back further still was "a back room which had doubtless at one time been used for a kitchen" but was "now occupied by tubs and refuse and is as dirty and ill-smelling a hole as one could wish to get into." The whole place was uncarpeted, the *Courier* added, and in some places the walls had just received a fresh coat of red paint.

The first discovery was made by Detective Jim Sullivan, a nineteen-year veteran of the police force, who had made his way back to the laundry room where a variety of clothes were drying on the line. Hanging among them were several sheets of fabric, torn strips of muslin ironing cloth which Sullivan thought bore a strong resemblance to the bit of material that had been wrapped around Marian's body. They were similar in texture and size, the *Courier* noted, "but the most convincing part of this cloth was its great similarity in quality and ripping which it had, as shown later by a comparison with the piece of muslin as taken from the child's body."

Detective Jerry Lynch, meanwhile, had gone back up to the second floor, which was divided into three partitioned rooms used mainly for storage. In one of these rooms he came across a satchel, and from it Lynch withdrew a number of items that piqued everybody's interest. In addition to a piece of rope, some twine and more strips of ripped fabric, the detective brought forth a pair of loaded .22 caliber revolvers and what the *Review* described as "enough cartridges to last a couple days of rapid fire."

Evening Times reporter John Bowen had gone upstairs as well, leading detectives to the tiny crawl space he'd explored the previous week and extracting from that cramped garret a bundle of old and worn newspapers. These were gone over and found to be from the years 1898 through 1901, and they too were set aside and catalogued as items of interest, Marian's body having been found wrapped in old and discarded pages of newsprint published roughly within that time frame.

"This begins to look serious, boys," stated Chief Cusack, leading his men back downstairs and into We's bedroom area.

A bed was pushed lengthwise up against the northern wall of that room, and kneeling down to inspect it Detective Malcolm Cornish noticed some red stains – "dark," the *Courier* noted, "like congealed blood" – dripping down the wall. From the *Evening News*: "A bed was torn apart, and in order to examine the mattress in the dusk of the room a match was lighted. Then a spot of some reddish liquid was found upon the wall paper back of the bed and dribbling in two thin streams to the mop board. The stains were dried, and resembled blood that had tricked down the wall. The stains were of a maroon color like blood about a week old."

"There was where that child was killed!" exclaimed Detective Cornish.

"That is blood alright," Chief Cusack agreed.

"Gentlemen," reporter Bowen interjected, calling everyone's attention across the room, "here is the most conclusive evidence so far."

His employer, the *Evening Times*, elucidated: "Mr. Bowen had found on a hook on the wall a white blouse shirt, We's shirt, and it bore many traces of fresh blood. There were several spots of blood on the sleeves, about the size of a pea, and the wristband of the right sleeve was turned up, or rather turned over twice. This was turned back, and a blotch of blood, about the size of a silver dollar, was found on the sleeve, concealed by the turning up of the wristband."

"I think we've got the man we've been looking for," Chief Cusack decided out loud. "These are the things we've been looking for. I dismiss all other theories and suspicions from my mind now."

The detectives had been in the house for less than ten minutes, and already they had amassed a considerable amount of what they interpreted as strong evidence that Charley We had abducted, killed and disposed of the missing Marian Murphy. As such, the chief gave the order for both We and the visiting Charley Sing to be taken into custody.

"What for?" demanded We, wincing as Detective John Devine applied the handcuffs, perhaps a bit more snugly than necessary.

"You know well enough what for!" Chief Cusack shot back, then directing his men to notify Superintendent Bull at headquarters.

"When placed under arrest he was snappy, brazen, insolent," the *Evening Times* noted of We, "but after the handcuffs were placed on his wrist the color in his face grew to a more yellowish tint." He wondered aloud who would tend to his laundry, and as he and Sing were led from the house We in particular appeared "crushed and silent." A small crowd was beginning to gather outside, and everybody watched in amazement as the two men were hauled off to the tenth precinct over on Niagara Street.

Captain Patrick Kilroy arrived at the Hudson Street address a short while later, and Chief Cusack filled him in on the exhilarating details of the search, expressing his confidence that the correct man had been taken into custody. The detectives, meanwhile, continued tossing the premises. "Detective Sullivan dug the cellar bottom with a spade," the *Evening News* reported. "The gas in the stoves were turned off to search the ashes for traces of the dress and shoes worn by the child. Every nook and crevice of the two-story building was searched from cellar to garret."

In a small closet, the *Review* wrote, one of the men discovered a copy of the Holy Bible, "well thumbed and used with the accused man's name in it." And, right next to that, detectives seized "a handsome opium pipe which had been used recently, judging from the odor." The smell of opium "was plain in the house," that paper wrote, and a number of letters were discovered which suggested "that though We has borne an excellent reputation for some years in that section of the city, he was in some way connected with the Grand Transoceanic and Continental Underground."

* * * * * *

Charley We, it would soon be learned, was the Americanized name of Chinese national Lum We, born around 1864 in Guangdong, which has since grown to become China's largest and most populous province. Located in the southeastern portion of the mainland, just about a hundred miles northwest of Hong Kong, the coastal province was – and still is – a major trading port responsible for a huge portion of commerce throughout south China.

The country that Charley We had left behind, however, was hardly the looming communist dictatorship that exists today. The modern Republic of China, in fact, would not come into existence until 1912, and its swift fall to communism would come only after more than two thousand years of imperial rule. Since 1644 the country had been under the governance of the Qing dynasty, and as of the early nineteenth century, just a hundred years earlier, China had boasted the world's largest economy and contained a full third of its population.

Slowly, though, Western influence had come creeping in and ripping at the fabric of society, casting the country into turmoil and ushering in what historians now regard as China's "century of humiliation." Opium, then one of Britain's most profitable commodities, was being illegally imported from India and traded out of Guangdong, and China's efforts at quelling its commerce were met with British military aggression. The First Opium War, lasting from 1839 through 1842, resulted in a crippling defeat for the Qing dynasty, with opium continuing to flood the market and the British seizing Hong Kong for their trouble.

China's loss to both Britain and France in the Second Opium War, fought between 1856 and 1860, resulted in it ceding basically all of Outer Manchuria to Russia, and with opium officially made legal the narcotic's strongly deleterious effects were now wreaking serious havoc across what was left of the land. Around that same time the Taiping Rebellion, a ferocious uprising against the Qing dynasty, had plunged the country into a brutal civil war that wound up claiming an estimated twenty million lives.

Charley We was around thirty-eight years old, it was approximated, and he had left China around the age of twenty, landing in America sometime around the year 1885. It is worth noting that the federally-enacted Chinese Exclusion Act, which officially prohibited the immigration of Chinese laborers, would have gone into effect three years prior.

We had arrived first in San Francisco, where a wave of anti-Chinese sentiment then seemed to be nearing a fever pitch. With the transcontinental railroad having been completed in 1869, the Chinese had outlasted their usefulness and therefore overstayed their welcome in the American west. San Francisco's Chinatown, meanwhile, had become an absolute hotbed of vice and illegal activity, with gambling parlors and houses of prostitution operating right alongside opium dens in appalling open-market conditions. In response to all this the hot-tempered Irish labor leader Dennis Kearney had formed the Workingmen's Party of California, and according to the *Buffalo Evening News* We had been forced to leave that city "for his health" not too long after arriving.

He had spent the next six years, that paper wrote, in the city of Chicago, although nothing further is known about his time there or how it was spent.

Since arriving in Buffalo a decade earlier, though, We had owned and operated a series of laundries on both the east and west sides of the city. "Since his arrival here he has stuck to the washboard with more than the ordinary washerman's luck," the *Evening News* reported, pointing to We's having struggled to prosper in that position. "Ten years generally suffice for Chinese laundrymen to accumulate a couple of thousand dollars upon which they can retire to China to become capitalists and even aldermen and councilmen," however "varying degrees of bad luck" had conspired to keep him tethered to that profession.

There were, by 1902, approximately forty Chinese laundries in operation throughout the city, according to a *Buffalo Evening Times* article from earlier in the year. The city's Chinese population, by that point, had dwindled to just seventy-six (on paper, anyhow), with much of it concentrated along Michigan Street between Clinton Street and Broadway, that corridor coming to be known as Buffalo's own little Chinatown. Aside from laundry services, many of the Chinese of Buffalo made their way running chop suey establishments in this area.

The local papers, in describing Charley We's physical appearance, were not overly generous (to be expected, perhaps, given the grue-some nature of his accused crime and the general sentiment toward the curious nature of foreigners). "Charley We is a short, round, greasy-looking, slant-eyed, pock-marked Chinaman," the *Evening Times* declared, fairly inviting its readers to envision something straight out of a horror story. And while the *Buffalo Courier* wrote that We was "not a thin man, and, on the contrary, is fat," by today's standards he was probably little more than pleasantly plump. This rather matched his "moon face," the *Evening Times* thought, "one of the roundest faces to be seen in the Chinese colony here."

Upon his arrival in Buffalo, the *Buffalo Review* reported, We had joined the local branch of the Chinese Order of Freemasons, which was "comprised of some of the wealthiest and most influential Chinese merchants" in the region. Its rules were stringent, that paper noted – "to become a member the Celestial must have certain social qualifications; his family must have attained a certain degree of importance; there must be a certain number of children in the family; there must be no records of crime charged to any of the family members and the religious belief must be that of the state" – and We is said to have attended its meetings above a laundry on the no-longer-extant Union Street in Chinatown. That space, the *Review* added, also doubled as the colony's "joss house," a customary Chinese place of worship.

Around five years earlier, the *Evening News* learned, We had begun attending a Chinese-oriented Sunday school on Rhode Island Street, that facility set up by a reverend at the Jefferson Street Church of Christ Disciples. We was one of about thirty pupils who had attended, and that paper later managed to catch up and speak with one of his former classmates there.

You Lee operated a laundry at 1291 Jefferson, and he told the *Evening News* that he recalled We from their time together there. "Yes, he go; but not many time," Lee stated. "He too busy. Beside, he live too far." But We was "always good Chilaman," he'd insisted, and he absolutely "no killee li'lle gel."

* * * * * *

Almost right away, prisoners Charley We and Charley Sing were transported to a more secure and more central location, Buffalo Police Department headquarters downtown on the Terrace.

The scene there was one of "jubilation and wild excitement," the *Buffalo Review* wrote, and the suspects were ushered straight into the office of Superintendent Bull. Bull was joined in the interrogation process by Chief Cusack, with First Assistant District Attorney Frederick Haller and Second Assistant District Attorney Willard Ticknor also sitting in on the interview. We and Sing were isolated and questioned independently of each other, with various detectives joining in at different times.

We was grilled for over two full hours, police assuring him of a lighter sentence if he were to come clean and confess. Still, the *Buffalo Courier* noted, the man "simply shook his head and declared himself innocent." When confronted with the spotted clothing and asked about what appeared to be blood stains dripping down his wall, We simply shook his head and insisted the substance had merely been paint. Some of the walls in We's home had just recently been painted red, that paper pointed out, and those materials were turned over to the chemist Dr. John Miller for microscopic analysis.

Eventually the prisoners were remanded to separate cells there in headquarters, and according to the *Buffalo Evening Times* the one We was assigned was "the one once occupied by [Leon] Czolgosz, the murderer of President McKinley." No official charges were filed at that time, the paper wrote, but the two men were "held on an open charge."

Meanwhile, back on Hudson Street, police there had continued their search of the property, focused specifically on finding Marian's missing items of clothing. "Every scrap of paper, every piece of laundry, and even the mattresses on the beds and the chimneys were inspected to see if a piece of the child's clothing could not be found," the *Courier* wrote, although nothing of the sort would reveal itself that evening. At 5 p.m. Chief Cusack decided to call off the search for the night, directing Captain Kilroy to lock up the house and also to assign a guard detail to stand watch overnight.

Word of the arrest had disseminated quickly throughout the city, the *Evening Times* noted, and "within an hour or two the streets in the vicinity of the laundry were black with people." By 9 p.m., in fact, that paper estimated that the crowd gathered out front of We's establishment had grown to around four thousand people, and the four patrolmen tasked with guarding it were, quite understandably, "alarmed by their demonstrations." There were the inevitable calls to handle things extrajudicially, wrote the *Evening Times*, but at the end of the day "nobody cared to take the initiative, and there was no movement of any sort." Still, and just to be safe, Superintendent Bull ordered his men to "close every Chinese laundry or store in the city, and to warn all Mongolians to keep off the streets, if they valued their lives."

Right away the police had contacted Cornelius Murphy, drawing him down to the tenth precinct to advise him of the laundryman's arrest, and also to question him further regarding any interactions he or his family may have had with Charley We. From there Cornelius made his way over to 285 Hudson, arriving there with Marian's older sister Angela in tow. Speaking to a *Courier* reporter, he confirmed that he had often sent his clothes to be laundered at We's place, and that Marian may have become acquainted with the man thusly.

Angela then addressed the crowd, the *Evening Times* reported, and the little girl "attracted attention in the crowd by stating that she used to visit the Chinaman's place and she told the police nearby that Charley We was a nice man and would not kill her little sister." Angela spoke with the *Courier* reporter as well, revealing that We was in the habit of enticing the little girls who came around his place with the promise of exotic trinkets and gifts. "He said he would give us Chinese nuts some time," she said. "When we went down there with papa's laundry he promised us the nuts. He told another girl that he'd put her in a nice box and take her to China, but he didn't."

Other neighborhood kids were in the crowd, and a bunch of them were keen to have their voices heard as well. All told eight youngsters approached the *Courier* man, each claiming to have "visited the Chinaman various times and that he had offered them Chinese nuts and sticks of candy and asked them to call again." Twelve-year-old Esba Goshorn, for instance, lived five doors down from the Murphys, and Charley We had once given her "a nice pretty Chinese pin." But when she'd gone back there earlier that morning, Esba claimed, We inexplicably just "shook a flatiron at her and chased her out of the front door."

Other concerned neighbors stepped forward as well, including a number of people who had witnessed Marian interacting with We on a somewhat regular basis, even entering his house a time or two. "Frequently on her way to the candy shop she would be hailed by the Chinaman and induced to stop and talk," the *Courier* wrote the following morning, "he on the outside looking through the window and she standing outside in the front yard. Then on occasions she would go in. In fact, it was asserted by the neighbors that the Chinaman had a custom of talking to young women."

For weeks the police's investigation had stagnated, grinding to a near-halt as every proffered lead dried up, fell through or otherwise evaporated. Then, all at once, a breakthrough – a cache of circumstantial evidence discovered in the nearby home of a foreigner, whose ways and customs were entirely alien to people in this corner of the world. These curious habits, police assured the papers, would have allowed someone such as We to have conducted himself without arousing much suspicion. "They state that Chinamen make a practice of purchasing old papers in which to wrap up laundry," the *Evening Times* pointed out. "Thread and clothesline are also important features of a Chinese joint, and the lust of the yellow men is one of their characteristics."

The *Buffalo Evening News*, for its part, ran an even more damning assessment of We: "He lived within a block of Marian's home. The child knew him and could be seized by him without exciting her alarm. She could have been whisked inside his door without detection on the cool evening when the child disappeared, and this would account for the reason why she was not seen anywhere else throughout that night. A Chinaman alone, the police argue, could carry the bundle containing the child's body to the lake without being stopped, the police and citizens being accustomed to seeing them carrying packages of laundry through the streets at nightfall. In addition, the police point to the low estimation in which children are held in the minds of Chinamen as well as the state of bachelorhood in which most Chinamen live in this country."

As various high-ranking police officials milled about in front of the laundry that evening, each of them gave a statement of some sort to the press. "The evidence secured today is enough to make it certain," Captain Kilroy beamed to the *Courier*, reviewing the list of evidence searchers had uncovered. "We think we have sufficient evidence to indict the man and convict him," added Superintendent Bull.

Only Chief Cusack displayed some measure of conservatism in his remarks, telling the *Courier*: "While I am confident we are in the way to a solution of the Murphy mystery I cannot say, as Chief of De-tectives, that we have the murderers of the child. I will say, however, that the evidence against the Chinamen is strong."

SEVEN

Due Diligence

C ome daybreak the following morning, July 2, police were right back at 285 Hudson Street, tearing Charley We's laundry asunder in search of proof that Marian Murphy had met her demise at that address.

"Every room, every closet, every corner, and every chimney was looked into," the *Buffalo Evening Times* wrote. "Floors were torn up and spades were applied to the yard in the rear of the house, but nothing of importance was turned up." From the *Buffalo Evening News*: "Every corner in which anything could have been hid was gone into and the search included the tearing up of flooring which appeared to have been recently disturbed, but nothing new was found and the case against We stands where it did last night."

The home's most distinguishing characteristic, the *Buffalo Courier* wrote, was its abundance of filth, with innumerable vermin running about in conditions that bordered on abject squalor. "Rats scampered across the attic and cellar floors when the detectives commenced to go through them," that paper reported. "The cellar was particularly dark and it became necessary to borrow a lantern from a liveryman in West Avenue in order to make the search complete. When the rats saw the lamp they lost courage and scampered away. In the excitement one of the rodents jumped upon and ran up the leg of a detective sergeant. Uttering a scream, the representative of 'the finest,' made a bolt for the door. In the meantime the rat sought safety in a hole in the wall."

At police headquarters, meanwhile, the county's two assistant district attorneys, Frederick Haller and Willard Ticknor, appeared to conduct a second interrogation of their chief suspect, Charley We. "Cowering in his cell and peering an anxious yellow face through the dark prison bars," wrote the *Courier*, "We passed a solitary, wordless imprisonment. When Mr. Haller called upon him in the morning, and while he was being brought upstairs and into the inquisition room, he obeyed with meek humility, saying not a word and casting his oval eyes cunningly about him."

When pressed to account for himself, the *Evening Times* reported, We instead clammed up and stonewalled his questioners, feigning incompetence with the English language in order "to evade a direct reply." From the *Courier*: "He immediately professed a dense ignorance of English, shook his head and smiled grimly. That was all they got out of the Chinaman, except that he insisted that the supposed blood found on the wall by the side of his bed was 'plaint.'"

The morning papers had announced the arrest, breathlessly recounting the raid on Charley We's home and place of business (or, as the *Courier's* headline put it, his "Chinese Laundry Slaughter Pen").

The evening papers did the same, and due to the frenzied level of anticipation much of that day's coverage was notably devoid of journalistic circumspection. "Marian Murphy's murderer is behind the bars," the *Buffalo Review* stated conclusively, its headline declaring the mystery "suddenly and unexpectedly solved."

The *Evening Times*, for its part, was loudly trumpeting its own role in bringing We to the attention of police, its star reporter John Bowen having taken it upon himself to nominate the laundryman as a viable person of interest. In fact, that paper wrote, it had been the *Evening Times*' dogged reporting which had "obliged the police to do more energetic work on this fiendish case" to begin with, and but for that aggressive coverage "the police would have dropped the case long ago."

The Murphy family seemed to agree. In a sidebar appearing in that evening's edition, a letter from the child's grief-stricken mother was reprinted in full, along with a brief postscript from her husband:

Norman E. Mack, Editor and Proprietor Buffalo TIMES.

Dear Sir – I wish to thank you and THE TIMES for what you have done to unravel the terrible mystery about our beloved child's disappearance and death. But for the good work done by your zealous reporter, Mr. John S.V. Bowen, I doubt whether the latest developments would have followed. On Tuesday, June 26th, Mr. Bowen asked Mr. Murphy and myself if there were any Chinese laundries in our neighborhood, and I told him she used to play near the laundry. Mr. Bowen at that time spoke of a vacant house at No. 20 Malta Place which had not been searched, and he started out to search the Chinaman's place. We read about the search he made, in THE TIMES of Tuesday, June 26th, and he is certainly entitled to all the credit for directing the attention of the police to the place and for urging the police to make another search of the place after our dear child's body was found.

I know that Mr. Murphy shares this belief fully and will join with me in sincerely thanking you and Mr. Bowen for your sympathetic efforts in our behalf.

MARY E. MURPHY.

I heartily and fully concur in this.

CORNELIUS V. MURPHY.

Having presented the issue of Charley We's guilt as essentially a matter of fact, the *Evening Times* article went on to state that, in and around the neighborhood, We enjoyed a "somewhat unenviable reputation, not belying his looks, for he is certainly a bad-looking Chinaman." One woman came forward to claim that We had once pickpocketed a friend of hers, and when confronted he'd let the pilfered items fall to the floor and pretended to have been uninvolved. A man named Bertram Levy told the paper that, around five years ago, We had offered him five dollars if he could procure for him the company of a willing female. "He asked me if I had a sister to bring her around," Levy recounted incredulously. "That's the kind of a villain he was."

Only the *Buffalo Evening News*, in its accounting of the arrest, saw fit to pump the brakes a bit. Its headline, in fact, acknowledged that the evidence gathered by police was far from conclusive, and that in truth officials were "not so sure that Charley We is the man who killed Marian Murphy." Concerning the alleged blood stains on the wall and on the fabric, that paper wrote, We's explanation that it had been paint "looked strong in the view of the partiality of Chinamen for that color in decorations and in view of the additional circumstances that Chinamen in America always do their own painting."

Still, according the the *Evening Times*, that evening saw the first random act of public retaliation against the city's Chinese – an early-twentieth century "hate crime," as it were, a clear reaction to the previous day's scandalous and sensational arrest. "A crowd of boys attempted to wreck the laundry of Sam Kin at No. 76 Morgan Street yesterday afternoon by shooting off giant firecrackers in the doorway and firing blank cartridges at the windows," the *Evening Times* reported. "A small fire was started caused by the firecrackers, which the Chinaman put out himself. Several windows were also broken."

* * * * * *

The next day Detective Cornish invited Cornelius Murphy to join him in the field, scouring the area around the Hudson Street laundry for any evidence tying Charley We to Marian's death. It was Thursday, July 3.

The vacant house at 20 Malta Place was still being scrutinized, with investigators zeroed in on the empty and boarded-up home as the likeliest location for the crime to have occurred. "We are positive the murder was committed within 500 feet of the Chinaman's house and in the same block," one high-ranking police official told the *Buffalo Evening Times*.

Along the way, the *Evening Times* wrote, "Mr. Murphy demonstrated that the route from the Chinaman's house on Hudson Street to the vacant house on Malta Place is not very difficult, although quite circuitous." Since We's arrest Cornelius had loudly professed his near-certainty of the laundryman's guilt, however as they walked he seemed to be engaged in a weighty reflection, wrestling suddenly with some measure of uncertainty on that score. "I hope they have got the right man," he was heard to remark out loud, "for I'd dreadfully hate to see an innocent man punished for this crime."

And while their walkabout failed to yield anything of any real value, a tip did come into the tenth precinct that morning that placed a man bearing We's resemblance in the immediate vicinity of Forest Lawn Cemetery the night after Marian had been taken. Eugene Hendricks lived on Niagara Street, and he had been riding an eastbound Forest Avenue streetcar that Wednesday night, June 18, when a Chinese gentleman had stepped aboard sometime around 9:30 p.m. He'd been wearing "a loose Chinese robe, with flowing sleeves," the *Evening Times* reported, and the implication was that the man may have been Charley We, perhaps in the process of dumping the girl's body in Swan Lake. On the other hand, the *Buffalo Evening News* pointed out, Hendricks did allow that "all Chinamen look alike to me."

As for Charley Sing, who had merely been visiting We's laundry at the time police had raided the place, it was decided late that morning by District Attorney Thomas Penney to have him released from custody for lack of any evidence linking him to the crime. Unlike police investigators, the *Evening Times* noted, DA Penney was convinced that Sing's "reticence and bland and innocent demeanor was proof positive of his nonconnection with the tragedy." Around noon he was brought from his cell up to Superintendent Bull's office, the *Buffalo Courier* reported, and as Sing stood to face his captor he "shook all over, seeming to be uncertain as to whether he was to be liberated or to be given over to an angry mob."

The release of Charley Sing, Superintendent Bull assured the papers, in no way diminished or dampered the case against Charley We, whose guilt police now seemed convinced of completely. "Sing's release from jail will not weaken our case at all," Bull told the *Courier*, for instance. "He was arrested and held simply because he happened to be in We's place when the house was raided. It had been our intention to let him go as soon as he told all he knew of We. He did this and we let him go."

As for Charley We, it was quickly being learned that he was well-known and generally well-regarded amongst the Chinese population of Buffalo, and upon his arrest members of that community had quietly gone about attempting to arrange for his assistance. "Chinese residents in Buffalo," the *Courier* proclaimed, "are much stirred up over the arrest and retention of one of their countrymen without the formality of a charge being placed against him." From the *Evening News*: "Since the arrest of Charles We it has developed that the Chinaman has several friends who believe him innocent, as he is entitled to be considered until he is proven guilty."

An official interpreter was brought in to ensure a clear line of communication between the police and We, and also to act as intermediary between prosecuting officials and the local Chinese community at large. Jim Lee was perhaps the most prominent and well-known of all the Chinese living in Buffalo – "the uncrowned king of Buffalo's little Chinatown," the *Courier* would name him in a profile piece later that year, "a prominent figure in the local chop suey belt" and "one of the best known characters in the city" – and in his capacity as such he was called upon to assist in moderating the affair.

Jim Lee, whose true name was Num Hule, had come to America in 1874. Like We, he was from Guangdong, China, and like We he had landed first in San Francisco before gradually working his way east. Arriving in Buffalo in 1891, the *Courier* wrote, he had promptly "amputated his queue, bought a suit of American garments and started to live the life of an American." Before long Lee had begun to prosper handsomely, taking a bride from a wealthy New York City family and operating a successful eating house at 477 Michigan Street.

Perhaps not all of Jim Lee's wealth and influence was accumulated by legitimate means, however. "'Slippery Jim' Lee was a trafficker of opium into Buffalo across the Canadian border," Buffalo historian Steve Cichon wrote in a 2018 entry in his online blog *Buffalo Stories*. "Under cover of darkness, he and his cohorts climbed into rowboats in Canada to take the drugs from across the Niagara River. Once on this side of the river, the drugs were taken to the Michigan Avenue Chinatown for distribution."

He was also, the *Courier* article mentioned, suspected of helping smuggle Chinese expatriates into the country illegally, however when asked about all this Lee simply "smiled one of his most persuasive smiles and all suspicion was immediately dispelled, for such a smile could only be born in innocence and expanded in guilelessness." At age fifty, that paper wrote, "Jim says he is a good Chinaman and declares that he has sidestepped the pitfalls of pipe-hitting and the allied seductive vices of the Celestial." He occasionally served as translator for both the police and federal courts, and via his storied philanthropy Lee was known to have "cleared up many a stormy day for brother Celestials in hard luck."

When approached by the *Courier* and asked to comment on the case, Jim Lee gave the following brief interview:

"Do you think that Wee is guilty?"

"No, I think him innocent," replied Lee, and he puffed his cigarette vigorously as if to add emphasis to his answer.

"Is it because the man arrested is a Chinaman that you think him innocent?" was asked.

"No, I don't think he did it. If him guilty I say so. I think he not guilty," sharply replied Jim Lee.

"Why do you think him innocent?"

"Oh, he not got what you call it? nerve to do it," said Jim.

"You think a Chinaman would not have courage enough to commit a crime like that charged?" was asked.

"No, I think that Chinaman would not have nerve to do that. If he did it he would run away. He would be on his way to Hong Kong. He not stay here as long as this. He would run out quick. He even afraid to owe a man a bill. He run away when he owe men money." And Lee laughed.

"Are all Chinamen cowards?" was asked.

Jim appeared not to understand the meaning of the word coward. When it was explained to him he said:

"They do nothing like that. They afraid."

He spoke with the *Evening News* as well, telling what little he knew of Charley We and reiterating his opinion that We could not have been Marian Murphy's killer:

"Lum We not friend of me," he said in preface. "He talk some 'bout me. I have not much to do with him. He come up Michigan street sometimes, but I not see him. All same I do what I can for him, for him not do this."

"What reasons have you for thinking he did not kill Marian Murphy?"

"If he do that he skip. All Chinamen they skip when they kill or do bad. All same as in New York and California, when do bad they skip."

"But he may have thought he got rid of the body and would not be caught."

"Chinaman could not take body to place where found," said Jim Lee. "Chinaman get caught, sure, yes. S'pose they go to Forest Lawn, where three Chinamen buried; s'pose they go in hack. All the same they get stopped by police. All hacks stopped if Chinamen in them. You find it harder for Chinaman to take bundle to Forest Lawn than other men."

Jim Lee meditated for a while. Then a grin spread over his features.

"What is that for?" he was asked.

"You see picture in paper yesterday of Lum We? That not picture of Lum We!"

"Whose was it?"

"That was picture of Charlie Hin. He live in Michigan street, and he have fits when he see his picture in paper as one who killed little girl."

As a member in good standing of the Chinese Order of Freemasons, the *Buffalo Review* pointed out, We was entitled to receive aid from his local chapter, whose rules stipulated that the organization must "support and assist its members in times of trouble." Once We's case was formally evaluated, the *Review* wrote, "Lee expects that the prisoner will have all the financial help in his defense which could be desired if the society has reason to think that he did not commit the crime himself."

Arrangements were made that very afternoon, in fact, with a defense attorney who agreed to review the case on a tentative basis, and to ensure that at the very least the accused was being afforded his due process. Hamilton Ward, Jr. was a 31-year-old lawyer, the son of one-time New York State Attorney General Hamilton Ward. Having received a legal education at his father's law practice in Belmont, a tiny village about seventy-five miles to the southeast, the younger Ward had relocated to Buffalo upon his admission to the bar association in 1892, right away being appointed assistant district attorney for Erie County.

He had served in that capacity for six years, until the country's sudden preoccupation with certain foreign affairs – specifically, Spain's barbarous treatment of the people of Cuba – prompted the United States to break with its long-standing policy of noninterference and intervene on the island's behalf. Ruled by Spain for over four hundred years, Cuba was then rife with rebellion and seeking its independence, and the Spanish were rounding up dissidents and placing them in concentration camps. The U.S. military had sent over a Navy ship, the USS *Maine*, to stand sentry in the Havana harbor and to watch over American business interests, and that ship's mysterious explosion in February 1898 prompted congress two months later to declare the official start of the Spanish-American War.

With that the call had gone out for volunteers, and citizens had turned out in droves to advance the interests of their country. The most famous of these was Theodore Roosevelt, whose unit, the Rough Riders, carried the day on numerous occasions over there, contributing heavily to the United States' emphatic defeat over Spain within the span of just several months, boldly marking the emergence of America as a military superpower. Far less prominent but every bit as enthusiastic was Hamilton Ward, Jr., who had rounded up some acquaintances from Buffalo and Belmont and signed on as part of a company unit. As commanding captain of that unit Ward had served with distinction from July 1898 through September 1899 in Pinar del Rio, Cuba, "where the fighting was the heaviest," according to his obituary in the *Buffalo Courier-Express*, and where he had "led his company into many of the engagements which caused the downfall of the enemy."

Upon his return to Buffalo in 1900 Ward had opened a private law practice, located downtown inside the Erie County Saving Bank building in Shelton Square, and quickly he had gained some measure of local prominence, specifically in his capacity as a trial attorney. He was, according to the reference book *History of the Bench and Bar of Erie County New York*, "a first-rate all-around lawyer, especially at home before a jury," and upon his agreeing to look into Charley We's case the *Review* pointed out that "Mr. Ward has handled successfully more Chinese litigation than almost any other lawyer in the city." What's more, the *Evening Times* noted, Ward had recently defended a one-time coroner on charges of "robbing the dead," so he was unlikely to be cowed by public outcry or criticism against him.

Ward would eventually rise to occupy the highest office in the state, following in his father's footsteps and being elected New York State attorney general in 1928, and he might have gone on to run for mayor of Buffalo had double pneumonia not claimed his life four years later at the age of sixty-one. A lifelong outdoorsman and conservationist, Ward would also help found and design both Allegheny State Park and Chestnut Ridge Park, bequeathing upon his death several hundred acres to the latter, which still bears a monument to his achievements and his contributions to the Western New York region.

The attorney paid a quick visit that afternoon to the tenth precinct, and from there he went to check out his client's laundry on Hudson Street. Arriving at We's establishment, the *Courier* reported, "Mr. Ward attempted to enter but was refused admission by the police on guard there." With this he called on Superintendent Bull at headquarters, requesting permission to consult with We in his cell, however Bull just referred him to District Attorney Penney up the way at City Hall. There Ward found that the DA was out of the office, and after enduring that whole frustrating runaround he apparently decided on the spot to accept We's case in a formal capacity.

With Charley We's acquaintances and countrymen loudly decrying his innocence, a counternarrative was swiftly bubbling up and police suddenly found themselves fending off allegations that they were attempting to railroad a potentially-innocent man, doing so for the express purpose of getting one of the city's most shocking and unpalatable unsolved cases neatly off its books.

"We are working on this because it is the likeliest clue that we have," Chief Cusack insisted to the contrary, speaking that afternoon with the *Evening News*. "If we find that the evidence we have secured amounts to nothing, we will say so." In fact, Cusack allowed, "the evidence secured certainly warranted the arrest, but whether it will warrant any arraignment remains to be seen."

* * * * * *

The following day was the Fourth of July, and despite the holiday attorney Hamilton Ward, Jr. headed down to police headquarters, where he was allowed in to meet and visit privately with his client, the Chinese laundryman and accused child killer Charley We.

"He says that he does not know the Murphy girl apart from the other children that played around the place," Ward told the papers that afternoon via a written statement declaring his representation of We. "He is horror-struck at the charge which I informed him had been made against him. He is confined under no lawful authority."

About a half a dozen friends and supporters also came to call on We at headquarters, the *Buffalo Courier* reported, however each of them was turned away and We was allowed "no visitors except the jailers who brought him his food." All of the prisoner's seized personal effects, as well as the remaining contents of his laundry, had been duly signed over to his legal representation, and Ward dispatched a representative to the Hudson Street address to shore up his client's property. Arriving there with Chinese immigrant advocate Jim Lee, the *Buffalo Express* wrote, that representative found that "the interior of the place has been practically torn to pieces by the police."

The police that morning had received yet another potential lead, this one coming from two men who operated a motorized rail trolley that ran up and down West Avenue. Michael McMorrow, the car's motorman, and William Clark, its conductor, presented at the tenth precinct stationhouse after reading in the previous day's papers the account of Eugene Hendricks, who had reported seeing a Chinese man toting a large bundle up near Forest Lawn Cemetery right after Marian had vanished. This had prompted the men to recall a similar incident they had taken note of around roughly that same time, although neither could be certain of the exact date.

At around 9:30 p.m. one night that week, McMorrow and Clark told Assistant District Attorney Frederick Haller, their car had picked up a Chinese gentleman at the corner of West and Hudson, a little over a hundred feet from We's laundry. He'd been traveling with a large clothes basket, apparently containing something of considerable weight, which he had placed upon the trolley's rear platform and monitored closely for the duration of his trip. Before stepping off with it at Forest Avenue he had requested a transfer, and another ride a mile and a half east along Forest would have delivered him to that street's terminus at Forest Lawn.

The presumption, the *Buffalo Evening Times* wrote, was that the basket the man had been carrying contained "the body of the murdered child and that he was on his way to the Delaware Avenue bridge over Scajaquada Creek, where the body was cast into the water." As a hypothetical this tallied loosely with citizen Hendricks' account of having seen a Chinese man aboard what would have been the second leg of that trip, however neither McMorrow nor Clark could say for sure that it had been that same evening, and furthermore the man seen by Hendricks had carried no such bundle.

All the same, police decided to do their due diligence and have the trolley men escorted down to headquarters, bringing each of them before We to see if either could identify him as their basket-hauling passenger. Neither could, as the night in question had been more than two weeks earlier and neither could have then foreseen being later called upon to make the distinction. "It struck me that the Chinaman we carried that night had a fuller, rounder face than this fellow," conductor Clark told the *Express* before leaving the building. "I can't tell much about that though, for it was some time ago and I had no reason for taking any special notice of the Chinaman." Motorman McMorrow put it more bluntly: "I can't tell one of those Chinks from another."

In all likelihood, it seems, the passenger described by witnesses McMorrow and Clark had not been Charley We, and apart from his nationality there had been no real reason to suspect the unknown man of anything nefarious whatever. And while they certainly appreciated the enthusiasm, police declared, it was hardly necessary for the good and well-meaning people of Buffalo to report each and every sighting of or encounter with an unknown member of the Chinese community.

"There is too much importance attached to seeing a Chinaman here and a Chinaman there," Chief Cusack told the *Buffalo Evening News* late that afternoon. "To my mind it would be more suspicious if there were no Chinamen seen at all in the street cars for the last two weeks. You see them every day. They have business calling them to different parts of the city daily, so why should they not be seen in the street cars?"

* * * * * *

The weekend upon them, authorities were hardly in a position to take a few days off and coast on the merits of their investigation. An official inquest was scheduled to take place Monday morning, the *Buffalo Evening News* reported, and "if the police and the District Attorney present a strong case against the prisoner he will be held for the grand jury. If not he will be formally discharged from custody."

When a *Buffalo Evening Times* reporter pointed out to District Attorney Penney that the sewer connected to Charley We's place had not yet been looked into, the DA promptly got in touch with Superintendent Bull and directed him to get it done at once. The house's "closet and sewer afforded a very convenient place to conceal the thing sought for by the police," that paper explained, "i.e., the clothes of the murdered child."

The term "closet," in those days, referred to what was essentially a small bathroom, and the *Evening Times* described the one in We's establishment as "the old-fashioned sort, not much better than a cesspool." In fact, the paper wrote, the man charged with its excavation that afternoon "stated that the closet is only drained by the rainfall and is one of the worse places of the kind he has ever seen on the West Side of the city."

Theodore Woodruff was a carter who lived at 399 Seneca Street, and he was tasked that Saturday afternoon with supervising the group of vault cleaners who arrived to open up and look through the sewer. "It is a great surprise," he marveled aloud, "to find such a place as this on the West Side. I didn't imagine there was such a vile place in the city." Work got underway around 1:30 p.m., but after just thirty minutes it became apparent that there was a limit to what the men would be able to accomplish. A thorough excavation, the *Evening Times* reasoned, would involve the sewer being opened up as far out as the sidewalk, a job which would require diggers and plumbers, so Superintendent Bull declared he would make the necessary arrangements and revisit the matter in the coming week.

Jim Lee, meanwhile, was running himself ragged advocating on Charley We's behalf, even managing to be allowed in to visit the prisoner in his cell at police headquarters. "He all broke up," Lee subsequently reported to the *Evening News*. "He was locked way down in cellar. Him plenty scared. Him not know what him locked up for." Lee also had been seeking someone to help manage We's business affairs, specifically with regard to the operation of his Hudson Street laundry, however no member of the Chinese community seemed particularly willing to step up and take the risk. "Nobody care go there," Lee explained. "Too much people 'round there when Chinamen look at place. All 'fraid to go. Place all tore up, too. Cost five hunner dollar to fix it. Awful dirty."

That reticence aside, the *Buffalo Courier* wrote, the Chinese of Buffalo stood firmly behind their accused countryman, and across the country colonies of Chinese expatriates were following the case with great interest. "Likewise," that paper wrote, "prominent Chinamen from New York and other cities are dropping into town, and though they cannot be gotten to say that they are here in connection with Charlie We's arrest, there is little or no doubt but what their mission here is in connection with We's case."

That evening, the *Courier* wrote, "a meeting of prominent local Chinamen was held somewhere in the vicinity of Michigan Street," and "matters pertaining to the arrest of Charlie We were taken up and discussed at length and steps taken to aid the accused Chinaman in every possible way." Attorney Hamilton Ward, Jr. was not present, however there was much talk of taking legal action against the authorities once We's innocence had been established. They intended to bring a suit against Chief Cusack for false arrest, and another against either Superintendent Bull or District Attorney Penney for false imprisonment. In addition to a separate charge of malicious prosecution, the *Evening News* wrote, "still another action may be brought for wrongful damage, for trespass and for conversion, all growing out of the raid upon We's laundry."

Another tip had come into the tenth precinct that afternoon, however it was precisely the type police had already declared to be of little value. Another motorman and another conductor, A.B. Streeter and James McDonald, respectively, reported to Captain Kilroy that they too had carried a Chinese passenger aboard their car, which ran up Forest Avenue, sometime around the night Marian had been kidnapped. "It is very probable," the *Buffalo Express* wrote, "that the Chinaman McDonald and Streeter refer to is the one who rode from Hudson street and West avenue upon the Grant street car as described by Conductor Clark and Motorman McMorrow."

This would have been at around 10 p.m., the witnesses approximated, and the man had gotten off right near the cemetery, although neither could recall whether he had carried with him a large laundry basket. "Streeter and McDonald were taken to police headquarters," the *Express* wrote, where "they saw Charley We and said it would be impossible for them to identify him as the Chinaman they carried."

With Monday morning's inquest fast approaching, police were scrambling to gather every last bit of evidence that might help implicate We and move his case before a grand jury. It was generally believed, the *Evening Times* admitted, "that the present evidence against We is inadequate to secure his conviction, although some of this evidence is of the strongest of circumstantial testimony possible to secure."

On the other hand, the *Courier* reported, there were rumors that "the police had been secreting facts and that when the case comes before the inquest something sensational is to be expected."

EIGHT

Legal Maneuvering

Monday, July 7, began bright and early at the morgue.

There convened that morning just about every major player involved in the ongoing Marian Murphy saga, each of them summoned to provide his or her testimony in the official inquest into the child's abduction and subsequent killing. The purpose of the inquest was to determine whether there existed enough evidence against Charley We, the Chinese laundryman held in connection with the crime, to warrant his continued incarceration.

"If the police and the District Attorney present a strong case against the prisoner he will be held for the grand jury," the *Buffalo Evening News* wrote in advance of the occasion. "If not he will be formally discharged from custody."

Held in the morgue's chapel, the proceedings commenced at 8 a.m. and were overseen by Police Court Justice Thomas F. Murphy, with witnesses called to the stand to substantiate the statements of fact as laid out by Assistant District Attorney Frederick Haller. The accused was present, with local attorney Hamilton Ward, Jr. appearing as his legal representation and Chinese community advocate Jim Lee on hand as translator.

The first to testify were Robert Troup and George McGill, the Forest Lawn Cemetery employees who had discovered Marian's body while closing up on the night of June 27. Each of the young men told of finding and fishing the girl's body out of Swan Lake, describing also the deteriorated condition of her remains and the tattered bundle that had encased them.

Erie County Medical Examiner Earl Danser was next to take the stand, and he also reviewed the conditions of the body at its finding, delving then into the specifics of his autopsy examination and reading aloud the report in full. Dr. Danser then fielded a series of clarifying questions, reiterating that it was his professional opinion that the Murphy child had met her demise via asphyxiation, probably secondary to strangulation.

Josephine Mumm, the Murphy family's domestic servant, was then called upon to recall the night of June 17, when Marian had last been seen by her or anybody else not responsible for the girl's death. Marian had cleared her plate and collected five cents, Josephine testified, before dashing out and refusing to stay indoors upon her return. She also told of later identifying Marian's body at the morgue, and in his cross-examination attorney Ward attempted to sow some measure of doubt in her ability to have done so with absolute certitude.

"How did you know that the body you saw was that of Marian Murphy?" Ward asked pointedly.

"By the toes," Josephine replied with confidence. "Marian had a peculiar kind of toes and I could never forget them. They were more characteristic than her fingers. I had been in the custom of bathing the child and that's the way I knew about her toes."

The next witness to be sworn was Cornelius Murphy, the father of the slain five-year-old, and he took the stand to recount the night of Marian's disappearance, telling also of viewing her deceased body several times at the morgue. "I recognized the corpse as that of my child," he stated. "There was no other child missing and that helped me to believe it was the body of my child. I examined the marked finger and found the scar. The hair was the same, also the shape of the head. When the body was exposed to view it looked just as my children do when asleep. I am satisfied it was my child I saw in the morgue."

Ten-year-old Emma McGinness was called to the witness stand, and she reviewed her trip with Marian to the Malta Place candy shop on the night she'd gone missing, explaining about the bike and the pennies and how Marian had gone running off ahead of her for no discernable reason. She had last seen her friend, Emma testified, at the corner of West Avenue and Pennsylvania Street about twenty minutes before giving up and going home around 9 p.m.

William Mahoney, the fourteen-year-old boy who had told police he'd seen Marian that same night at around 8:45 p.m., told of his encounter that evening. "I was at The Front the night she was lost," he stated for the record. "I returned by way of Pennsylvania Street and Plymouth Avenue. I saw Marian turn the corner there. She went down Plymouth Avenue towards Hudson Street. Then I went home."

Judge Murphy was due shortly on the bench over in another court, so a little before 10 a.m. the proceedings were adjourned and set to resume at 2 p.m.

The tenth precinct's Detective Malcom Cornish was the first witness called after the break, and he was presented with the square of cloth found wrapped around Marian's body, as well as a knotted portion of the rope which had been used to tie her up. Detective Cornish confirmed that these were the items he had logged into evidence following the discovery of the girl's body, and the tenth precinct's Detective Sergeant Hugh Kennedy was then called up to provide confirmation of the same.

Chief of Detectives Patrick Cusack was up next, and his testimony was the most highly-anticipated of all the participants to that point. He recounted the July 1 arrest of Charley We and the subsequent search of his Hudson Street laundry, and again the cloth and the rope were presented for comparison. In response Chief Cusack produced a bit of rope he had seized from We's place on that occasion, passing the items to the judge and inviting his Honor to gauge their similarity for himself.

Attorney Ward then interjected, challenging the chief's authority to have executed the raid on his client's property.

"By what authority did you make the search?" Ward asked. "Did you have a warrant?"

"I had no warrant," Cusack conceded. "I made the search on my own authority."

At this Judge Murphy spoke up, reminding Ward that this was an inquest and not a formal legal proceeding, and that he had been granted permission to appear that day strictly as a courtesy. "It was then agreed between Mr. Ward and Mr. Haller that the question of authority should not be brought out," the *Buffalo Express* wrote, "but should be let to the outcome of a civil suit if such a suit should ever be brought."

It was chemist Dr. John Miller who turned out to be the star witness of the afternoon, and his followed the testimony of Chief Cusack. Dr. Miller's chemical and microscopic examination of the evidence – the materials found adorning Marian's person, as well as the items seized at the time of the arrest – was ongoing and taking place in another part of the morgue, and he was called up to speak to his findings thus far.

An official accounting of the contents of Marian's stomach, Miller said, had yet to be completed, however a preliminary analysis had suggested that the girl's final meal had consisted of meat and potatoes. This squared neatly with the testimony of Josephine Mumm, who had sworn to having served the Murphy family a supper of liver and bacon, as well as a side of potatoes, on the night Marian had gone missing. "This established the probability that the child had been murdered on the same night she was abducted," the *Buffalo Courier* wrote.

Dr. Miller had also examined thoroughly the sheet of ironing cloth found wrapped around Marian's body, comparing and contrasting it with the one taken from the valise in Charley We's attic. And while both were similar in size, shape, texture and appearance, the piece preserved from the discovery scene measured seventy-two threads per square inch, while the sample from the laundry had a thread count of just sixty-eight. When asked by the judge if ten days in the water might have resulted in the fabric having shrunk, Dr. Miller stated that he could not be certain one way or the other.

With regard to the stains on each piece of fabric, however, the chemist was able to provide a more definitive answer. None of those stains had been made by blood, Miller said, and the markings on each had instead been left by indelible ink, or marking ink. This was generally regarded as the most significant fact to be learned that day, and certainly one which would help bear out the defense's case that the accused had been uninvolved and wrongfully arrested.

Michael McMorrow and William Clark, two of the men who had reported seeing a Chinese fellow aboard a trolley shortly after Marian's abduction, then took the stand and gave their accounts, although pretty much everything out of each of them was awash with doubt and uncertainty.

"Will there be evidence shown tending to hold any particular person?" attorney Ward asked finally, adding a flourish of theatrical exasperation.

"There will be," ADA Haller assured him.

"All right," replied Ward. "The reason I asked is because there is a Chinaman locked up whom I want to get out if there is to be no charge placed against him, that's all."

It was around 3:30 p.m., and having listened to the accounts of thirteen different witnesses Judge Murphy was ready to make his ruling. In light of all the coincidences and similarities, he stated, it was not unreasonable to issue an arrest warrant and lodge a formal charge against the accused.

As such, a warrant was drawn up charging laundryman Charley We with murder in the first degree, and Judge Murphy scheduled the matter to be heard the following morning in police court.

* * * * * *

The next day – Tuesday, July 8 – Charley We was formally arraigned in police court, which was held in a small courtroom at police head-quarters downtown.

Having overseen the previous day's inquest, Police Court Justice Thomas Murphy now presided over the arraignment proceedings, calling his court to order around 10 a.m. and sending for the prisoner to be brought in. The courtroom was packed with spectators, the *Buffalo Evening Times* reported, including "several Chinamen with their queues hanging down their backs," and attorney Hamilton Ward, Jr. again appeared to argue in We's defense. A number of police detectives were also in attendance, however conspicuously absent from the occasion was Cornelius Murphy or any other member of the Murphy family.

We was ushered into the courtroom by Detective Jim Sullivan of headquarters, who had been present at the man's arrest and a participant in the subsequent search of his premises. Sullivan was adamant in his belief that We had murdered the child, and much of the 49-year-old detective's zeal was likely borne of a keen sympathy for the grieving Murphy family – Sullivan and his wife Hannah had, by that point, lost four children of their own, and he knew too well the unique sting of losing a young one.

The defendant was attired in traditional Chinese garb – a loose-fitting tunic and an oversized black coat, topped off by a steel-colored fedora. "We entered the court room smiling and as jaunty as if going to a Sunday-school picnic," the *Evening Times* declared, categorizing his behavior as both "crafty" and "foxy" and suggesting further that he seemed to be "playing possum with the police." The accused "preserved his characteristic Mongolian sang froid as he took the prisoner's dock," the *Buffalo Evening News* wrote, and the *Buffalo Review* noted that We "exhibited considerable indifference" and "apparently had little interest in what was going on."

"Charley We," began Judge Murphy, "you are charged with murder in the first degree in that on or about the 17th day of June, you did feloniously and with deliberate intent to kill, cause the death of Mary A. Murphy by strangulation. You may be examined here or by indictment. How do you plead, guilty or not guilty?"

"Not guilty," attorney Ward replied, entering a plea on his client's behalf.

Assistant District Attorney Frederick Haller then requested a two-day adjournment, and the judge set the matter down to be revisited on Thursday, July 10. The intervening two days, he announced, would afford Dr. John Miller additional time to examine further the material evidence in his possession, as it was believed that a closer chemical analysis might yet reveal trace amounts of washed-out blood.

At this Ward interjected, insisting that if any further testing were to be done he wanted a second, independent chemist allowed to oversee the process and to represent We's interests accordingly. From the *Evening News*: "Chemist Miller said he did not care whom Mr. Ward named to work with him, provided he did not name a certain man. In order to avoid this contingency he whispered the name in Mr. Ward's ear. The name was overheard and occasioned a laugh."

At the conclusion of the arraignment We was escorted back to his jail cell, and his attorney remained on hand to speak briefly with the papers.

"I am all ready for the examination," Ward stated in response to a question from a *Review* reporter. "In fact, I was ready when the warrant was issued yesterday afternoon."

* * * * * *

A curious thing transpired the following afternoon, with prisoner Charley We being retrieved from his cell and once again brought before Judge Murphy to be rearraigned on precisely the same charge.

"Mr. Ward found Justice Murphy in the Police Court a few minutes after 1 o'clock," the *Buffalo Express* related. "He explained that he had decided to have his client waive the examination scheduled for [tomorrow], preferring to have the case presented direct to the grand jury. Justice Murphy said the prisoner had that right."

This was somehow coordinated without proper notice being given to the district attorney's office, and a short while later Detective Jim Sullivan brought We back upstairs and parked him in the prisoner's box. "During the entire proceedings," the *Buffalo Courier* wrote, "We stood in front of the judge's bench, hat in hand. He did not utter a word. That peculiar grin appeared on his face and remained there."

Attorney Ward announced his intent to waive his client's right to an examination, originally scheduled to take place the following day. A grand jury was currently convened – although nearing the end of its session – and Ward wanted it to consider We's case before being disbanded for the summer. Ward was certain that, based on the scant evidence produced at the inquest, the grand jury would decline to hand down an indictment and his client would quickly be exonerated.

"I desire to plead not guilty to the charge of murder in the first degree, waive examination and have the case go before the present grand jury," Ward told the court. "I believe that all the evidence was taken at the inquest, and do not wish to cause any delay and have the case put over until the next session of the grand jury."

"Very well," Judge Murphy responded. "We, you are committed to jail to await the action of the grand jury, without bail."

Charley We, to this point, had been kept in a tiny cell at police headquarters – "the Freezer," it was called – and "his confinement there," wrote the *Buffalo Evening News*, "while it did not lead him to talk to the police, told on his health somewhat and when he was arraigned in Police Court the first time he was slightly nervous and paler than when arrested." Now, with the accused remanded to custody pending the action of a grand jury, Judge Murphy ordered him transferred to a larger and more long-term holding facility.

The Erie County Jail, at the northwest Delaware Avenue and Church Street, was an imposing, four-story building with the capacity to accommodate up to two hundred prisoners. Built in 1877, the jail had most famously housed the presidential assassin Leon Czolgosz, who had spent a bit of time there awaiting trial in the fall of the previous year. It has since been demolished, replaced in 1938 by the Erie County Holding Center, which stands roughly in that spot today.

The jail was a five-minute walk up the Terrace, and it fell to Detective Sullivan to transport the prisoner there on foot, quietly and hopefully without incident. "Detective Sullivan, who had charge of We, placed the handcuffs on We's right hand and locked the other cuff about the wrist of his left arm and started for the jail with his prisoner," the *Evening News* reported. "There were few persons on the street at the time," the *Buffalo Evening Times* added, "and the journey was accomplished in safety. Detective Sullivan was well prepared in the event of a demonstration."

Directly across Delaware Avenue from the jail stood the county courthouse, and attorney Ward hastened there from police headquarters, appearing around 2:15 p.m. before Erie County Justice Edward K. Emery in an apparent attempt at an end run around the district attorney's office. There he made a rather impassioned motion requesting Judge Emery to direct the sitting grand jury to take up We's case immediately, arguing that his client would otherwise be forced to spend the remainder of the summer unjustly imprisoned, as its next session was not scheduled to convene until the second Monday in September.

His offices were in the same building, so it was inevitable that District Attorney Thomas Penney should catch wind of Ward's shifty ploy and come hurrying over to Judge Emery's courtroom. This, the *Evening News* reported, led to "a warm argument before the Court," with Ward citing section 260 of the New York State Code of Criminal Procedure, which stated that an empaneled grand jury must consider the case of any man presently imprisoned on a criminal charge who has not yet been indicted.

"I want to say that the grand jury now in session will be discharged this afternoon," DA Penney stated in reply. "It has already been in session two weeks longer than the usual time, and the jurors have already made objection to the unusual length of time they are being required to sit. It isn't fair to keep them here so long. Some have important business interests to look after. Only today a number of them asked me to state to the court that they would like to get away. All the cases prepared up to the present time. have been presented to the jury. Its work is finished, and the plan is to have the jury discharged either this afternoon or tomorrow morning."

"The law," Ward shot back, "is supposed to guarantee to every man certain rights, whether he be a Chinaman or a railroad president. One of those rights is that of having charges against him presented to a grand jury as soon as possible after he has been held. The We case could be presented to the grand jury in two hours, if one may judge by the time required in the presentation of testimony at the inquest."

Ward went on like that for a bit, the *Express* wrote, until eventually DA Penney "showed some heat."

"What kind of a scheme is this, anyway?" he finally erupted. "Why did Mr. Ward get things changed in this way, unexpectedly, unusual, unprecedented? In plain language, the facts in the case are that he wants to take the police by surprise so that they can't develop their case against him. He thinks that if the case goes to the grand jury now his man will be discharged because the evidence is not in shape. Perhaps he is afraid that if the man is held until fall the police will, during the summer, find evidence of such a nature that there will be no escape for him. If you let him go now, and should it be learned that he is beyond question the guilty man, where will you be in the fall?"

In the end Judge Emery denied Ward's application, refusing to impede the dismissal of the present grand jury and remanding Charley We to the county jail for at least the next two months. The dejected attorney then asked to at least be allowed to draft a note to the grand jury, a hastily-scrawled letter pleading with its members to consider the facts of his client's case, which DA Penney agreed to hand-deliver.

At 4 p.m., however, the grand jury convened at the county court-house to read its final report, and in it there was no mention of the case against Charley We.

"The case now stands for the September grand jury," the *Evening Times* wrote, "which will convene on the 8th of the month. This will give the police, the chemist and the prosecuting office ample time to work on the case."

NINE

A Chinaman's Chance

Freshly remanded to the Erie County Jail, prisoner Charley We wasted little time in getting acclimated to his new surroundings.

Compared to the desolate holding cells at police headquarters, the *Buffalo Evening News* observed, his new accommodations were a significant upgrade, a big improvement in terms of space and general living conditions. Here, the paper wrote, We was "confined with the 60-odd other prisoners who are allowed the liberty of the jail pit for the greater part of the morning and afternoon," and he was "treated just the same as other prisoners awaiting trial or action of the grand jury."

In contrast to the protracted periods of isolation afforded him at headquarters, We was now flush with company and he immediately fell in with the other Chinese nationals being held there. There were thirteen other Chinese prisoners, most of them awaiting extradition proceedings, and they had been "pleased to welcome a fellow coun-tryman and did not care whether he was charged with murdering Marion Murphy or with a dozen murders," the *Evening News* wrote. "They made him at home immediately."

Now fourteen strong, the Chinese contingent ate together and traveled together as a pack, often playing cards and united constant-ly as they whiled away their time. "They chat together, walk up and down the granolithic floor together, play harmless fan-tan together and have a pretty good time for prisoners," the *Evening News* report-ed. "In one respect they are better off than their white fellow-pris-oners. They have good chop suey and tea to drink." We became es-pecially friendly with one man in particular, and the two quickly "struck up a warm friendship" and became "almost inseparable." Like We the man had come from Guangdong, and like everyone else who got to know We personally he was entirely convinced of the man's innocence. "Hlim too glood a fellow to kill girl," the man told the *Evening News.* "Him told me he didn't."

Right away, however, We's friends and acquaintances on the outside started turning up at the jail as well, leaving care packages filled with items meant to bring some measure of comfort and also to help lessen the sting of incarceration. "Charlie's packages have in several instances contained fine brands of tea, imported by Chinese merchants, and considered a dainty by the Celestials in the United States," the *Evening News* wrote, and occasionally the parcels would contain cigarettes or "queer Chinese tobaccos." These he shared with his tribe, and "in this manner each manages to have a little of the good things brought from the outside."

All told, and despite his confinement to the county jail for a min-imum of the next two months, the enviously unflappable Charley

We seemed jovial nonetheless – "as contented and care free as a Chinaman can be while away from his native land of rice fields, opium and pagodas," the *Evening News* remarked. In fact, that paper's reporter thought, since his change of venue "We has improved in spirits and looks now as though the prospect of several weeks in jail before his case can be presented to the grand jury does not worry him at all."

* * * * * *

Charley We's ongoing incarceration bought investigators some time, but in order to make a first-degree murder charge stick police knew they needed to turn up some tangible evidence, and it needed to happen before the case went in front of the September grand jury.

The *Buffalo Courier*, on July 9, had issued a sensational report claiming that Dr. John Miller, the chemist working on behalf of the county, had further examined the cloth found about Marian's body as well as a section of wallpaper removed from We's bedroom, and he had determined conclusively that the spotting on each had been made by human blood. "Chemist Miller reported this fact to police yesterday," the paper indicated, "but the information was not made public, and it has been the intention of the officials to withhold it until the prisoner was actually placed on trial for his life."

In truth, however, that entire bit had been a complete fiction, an utter fabrication designed to further sensationalize the already-scandalous matter. And Dr. Miller, when he read it, rather hit the roof. "I think that the reporter who wrote that would better quit hitting the pipe," he sniped angrily to a *Buffalo Evening News* reporter later that afternoon. "I mean it. What I have said expresses my views exactly concerning that statement and the one who wrote it."

The following day – Thursday, July 10 – police reconvened at Forest Lawn Cemetery, fanning out in search of Marian's dress or any of the clothing she'd been wearing at the time of her abduction, the district attorney's office having no doubt impressed upon them the dire importance of their locating such an item.

Chief Cusack and Captain Kilroy, along with a pair of tenth precinct detectives, spent the morning dragging Swan Lake and nearby portions of Scajaquada Creek, fervently hoping to dredge up anything at all tying We to the crime. Using "a line attached to which were 20 fishhooks," the *Evening News* wrote, the men "brought to the surface practically every movable object on the bottom of the creek and lake." They found, however, "no trace of the clothes which the child wore when she disappeared, nor anything else which would shed any light on the mystery surrounding her disappearance and death."

That afternoon, back on the city's west side, a pool of officers gathered at 285 Hudson Street, We's laundry, compelled by the DA's office to complete an extensive search of the sewer there. Workers had done a perfunctory job of opening it up the previous Saturday – and it had been declared clear and unobstructed on that occasion – but they had only done so where the sewer met the house and a proper search would involve clearing the length of pipe as it extended all the way out to the trap near the street.

Around 2:30 p.m., according to the *Evening News*, Chief Cusack and Captain Kilroy were joined by two other detectives, and they looked on as work began under the supervision of Patrick J. Kennedy, the city's deputy street commissioner. "Every inch of the sewer," that paper wrote, "from the vault in the rear to the street, was examined," and it was quickly learned, added the *Buffalo Evening Times*, "that the sewer was clogged up despite the report of the police to the contrary."

From the *Evening News*: "The trap in the front yard was uncovered and lifted out of place. It was closely examined by Chief Cusack and Capt. Kilroy, and found to be clogged with sewage. No particle of the dress was found in it. The trap beneath the closet in the rear of the house was likewise examined without result. Then the street employes affixed a wooden ball five inches in diameter to one end of a number of laths fastened together and pushed it through the six-inch sewer, clearing the latter to the point where the trap was taken out in the front yard. The sewage thus collected was taken out and examined on the grass by Chief Cusack and Capt. Kilroy. The search failed to lead to the discovery of any portion of the dress sought for."

The uncomfortable truth, however, as the *Buffalo Review* correctly pointed out the following afternoon, was that the county's case against Charley We was, in all but superficial appearances, weak and dying on the vine. "It is generally admitted," the *Review* wrote, "that there is not the slightest legal evidence upon which to hold him," and that "it requires no legal training to realize that it is a mighty slim case." This was something of an about-face for that paper, and a far cry from the tenor of its coverage of We's arrest, at which time it had referred to the accused laundryman, definitively, as "Marian Murphy's murderer."

The *Evening Times*, on the other hand, was still tying itself in knots trying to help further the prosecution's case, fairly scraping the bottom of the barrel in terms of raking up new material to provide fresh ongoing coverage. In its expanded edition of Sunday, July

13 (the paper published Sundays as the *Buffalo Illustrated Times*), it was announced that "palmistry has come into the Murphy case," with one "well-known local palmist" making a concerted effort to obtain impressions of Charley We's palms. "In the case of all noted criminals," the paper claimed, "the palm, when examined, has shown pronounced traces of traits which would naturally lead up to the sort of crime committed."

Police had denied the palm-reader access to their prisoner, so instead of We's prints that oracle had had to make do with those of two other members of the local Chinese colony. It took a bit of cajoling, but eventually two of We's former Sunday school classmates, Lee Dein and Young Chong, consented to having their impressions taken, and these were reproduced and carried alongside the *Illustrated Times* article. "While no deductions of value can be drawn from hands, other than those of We himself," the paper allowed, "it may be interesting to note that the palmist in question says that from a general study of hands of the Chinese which he has made, he feels safe in saying that the members of the Chinese race as a rule, show in their palms, such traits as would lead one to expect crimes of the Murphy type from them."

Barrister Ward, however, was hardly content to sit back all summer and allow things to fall into place once September rolled around. "I do not think there is one bit of direct evidence which warrants the prosecuting officials of this city to hold my client through the summer months," he told the *Courier* on July 15, speaking from his office as he prepared yet another legal motion aimed at securing We's immediate freedom. "All the evidence that has been produced is purely circumstantial and of an indirect kind at that."

Specifically, the paperwork Ward was drawing up was a petition for a writ of habeas corpus, seeking immediate action based on his client's fundamental Constitutional right to be safeguarded against unlawful detention. A writ of habeas corpus, if accepted, states that a prisoner must be brought before a state Supreme Court justice, and that justice shall then rule solely on the issue of incarceration, with the option of setting the defendant free right then and there on the spot.

The application was to be delivered the following morning before New York State Supreme Court Justice Daniel J. Kenefick, a former Erie County district attorney who had ascended to the state's highest bench three years prior, and Ward spent the afternoon in the presence of a stenographer readying his case. "The opportunity to secure We's release, I feel confident, is very good," he told the *Courier*.

* * * * * *

At 10 a.m. the next morning Ward appeared in Special Term of New York State Supreme Court, held inside the County and City Hall building on Franklin Street downtown, where he formally submitted his typewritten petition to Judge Kenefick. Ward's argument, essentially, was two-fold – one, that Police Court Justice Thomas Murphy had lacked jurisdiction to issue the arrest warrant for We, with no directly incriminating evidence having been produced at the inquest, and two, that We was entitled to be discharged simply in light of the previous grand jury's failure to indict him.

Judge Kenefick, after reviewing the documents and determining that Ward's paperwork was in order, accepted the application and placed the case on the docket for the following morning at 11 a.m. His order, specifically addressed to Erie County Sheriff Francis T.

Coppins, mandated that the prisoner must be produced and brought before the court at that time. After speaking briefly with some reporters, Ward gleefully made his way from Judge Kenefick's courtroom to the offices of District Attorney Thomas Penney, bringing him up to speed and providing him with a copy of the judge's order.

The *Buffalo Evening Times* was on hand for all this, and in the crowd of courtroom onlookers its eagle-eyed reporter had taken note of at least one familiar face: "The most interested spectator before Justice Kenefick, while Attorney Ward was making his application for the discharge of the accused Chinaman, was Cornelius V. Murphy, the father of the murdered child. Mr. Murphy was not noticed by Mr. Ward, the court or any of the 50 or more persons present. He went away quietly while Mr. Ward was talking with the reporters."

At the appointed hour the following morning – Thursday, July 17 – all parties convened in Judge Kenefick's courtroom, the habeas corpus proceedings commencing a bit late due to a few equity cases taking precedent. Attorney Ward arrived, his clerk toting along nine big law books, with DA Penney and ADA Haller following closely behind. The case was called at 11:15 a.m.

A "rush of spectators" crowded the tiny courtroom, the *Evening Times* reported, including the murdered girl's father, who once again stood silently at the back of the cramped room observing the proceedings. "The announcement that the case would be argued," the *Buffalo Evening News* wrote, "had the effect of crowding the court room with morbidly curious people, mostly men, who seemed hopeful that the hearing would develop something new in the now famous murder mystery." The *Buffalo Courier*, however, countered that "a great many women were present and tried in every imaginable way to gain admittance to the room."

As for the defendant himself, Charley We had been retrieved from his cell at the county jail and hustled across the street, brought into the building and ushered past the waiting crowd gathered there in the courthouse corridor. "We was not handcuffed," the *Courier* noted, "but a couple of deputies brought up the rear. The law officers were on the lookout for any demonstrations against the prisoner. He was hurried through in double quick time. He had an expression of blank amazement on his face. His small eyes glanced furtively about and it was evident that he felt a great deal better when he was seated in a comfortable chair in the courtroom."

The case was called at 11:15 a.m., and Ward, who was nothing if not ardent about his client's defense, launched right into an impassioned presentation arguing the wrongful imprisonment of the accused laundryman. After citing the known and established facts of the case, the attorney began reviewing the testimony of police, witnesses and various experts given at the murdered girl's inquest. "Continuing," the *Evening News* reported, "Mr. Ward criticized in caustic terms the action of the District Attorney's office in seeking to keep We in jail all summer," and he concluded by proclaiming that "there is absolutely no evidence against this Chinaman. The Chinamen in Buffalo have not committed any crime, except that of smuggling."

Once attorney Ward had completed his argument Judge Kenefick called his court into a brief recess, wishing to hear another case and adjourning the matter until 2:30 p.m.

After the break ADA Haller spoke on the people's behalf, and he spent the next hour rebutting the defense's contentions point by point, reasserting the county's position that everything had been done according to the letter of the law. He also made much of lawyer

Ward's ill-fated decision to waive his client's right to examination, a reckless roll of the dice which now saw him seeking relief from his own actions.

"The prosecuting officer," Haller told the court, "is somewhat embarrassed by such an argument as that made by Mr. Ward, who almost assumes that the District Attorney is the jailer, or that the District Attorney is on trial here. Mr. Ward knows that the arrest of We was made by the police, that the District Attorney was not notified until after We's arrest."

The ADA then produced the bits of rope and cloth that had been found about the body, as well as the similar items police had seized out of We's laundry. "As he spread them out on the table," the *Courier* wrote, "We's blinking black eyes darted curiously at them. He bit his nails nervously and occasionally glanced from the articles on the table to Mr. Haller's face. Many of the women in the courtroom turned their faces away as Mr. Haller flaunted the evidences of the crime, and one woman wept. All eyes in the courtroom were turned to the Chinaman."

Judge Kenefick's ruling came not long after that, and having given the matter due consideration he summarily dismissed the writ of habeas corpus, dashing all hopes for We's release on that occasion. "In dismissing the writ," the *Courier* explained, "the court held that there was enough evidence to justify the Police Justice to issue a warrant and that if the defendant wished an examination he should have insisted on one at the time that We was arraigned."

We, meanwhile, "leaned forward with a face as immobile and waxen as a graven image as he heard Justice Kenefick speak the few words that sent him back to the County Jail, where he will stay until the September grand jury meets."

* * * * * *

The following day was Friday, July 18, and had she lived Marian Murphy would have been at home celebrating her sixth birthday, enjoying the summer with her parents and her three siblings, perhaps marking the occasion with a trip to a nearby drug store for an ice cream soda or something along those lines.

Instead, the *Buffalo Evening Times* received on that date a gut-wrenching transmission from the dead girl's eight-year-old sister Angela, who had chosen to mark the occasion by penning a quick note lamenting Marian's stolen innocence and also including a small bit of cash. The *Evening Times* reprinted her brief letter in full:

> City Editor TIMES:
> This is my sister's birthday and I am nearly heartbroken over little Marian's terrible death. Now she is a little martyr standing before God's throne pouring out from the depths of her affectionate heart fervent petitions for those who are sorrowing for her here below. Enclosed you will find my subscription, which you will kindly add to the memorial fund.
> JANE ANGELA MURPHY.

The memorial fund she referenced was an effort undertaken recently by the *Evening Times*, a collection that had started informally after a number of area schoolchildren began sending in small unsolicited donations. These selfless contributions, the paper had announced, would be pooled and used to fund an engraved tablet to be placed at Marian's gravesite, and donations ranging from a few cents up to a dollar or two had been pouring in daily ever since.

"Little Marian had four pennies in her hand the night she met her death," the *Evening Times* wrote, just as countless little girls across the city have four pennies of their own to part with, "and it is with these that the children who have started the movement for a school children's memorial tablet hope to erect it." On July 21 the paper announced that a total of fifteen dollars had been taken up thus far, pledging that "when the amount reaches $25 a committee of those subscribing will be formed to purchase the tablet and place it on Marian's grave in Holy Cross Cemetery."

Over a week went by, with no significant developments or news updates and with Charley We just languishing at the county jail, lost in games of mahjong and Fan-Tan and undoubtedly counting down the days until September. On Thursday, July 31, however, attorney Hamilton Ward took yet another run at winning his client's liberty, applying once again to New York State Supreme Court Justice Daniel Kenefick and requesting that We be released on his own recognizance.

Ward recently had tracked down an associate of We's, a Chinese fellow named Yep Jui, who had confirmed that the valise found in We's attic – the satchel containing the cloth and the rope now entered into evidence against him, as well as the two .22 caliber revolvers – actually belonged to him, and he was willing to attest to this on the record. Jui signed a prepared affidavit, the *Evening Times* reported, and in it he stated "that the bag found at Charlie We's house containing the tell-tale cloth and rope is his property and that its contents also belong to him. He says that the bag had been left by him at We's place for upwards of a year."

Judge Kenefick entertained Ward's petition on Thursday, July 31, and once he had completed his argument Assistant District Attorney Frederick Haller delivered his rebuttal, advising that police had lately turned up additional bits of evidence and arguing fervently against We's release. A witness had come forward, he stated, claiming to have seen Marian walking directly toward the defendant's laundry on the night she'd vanished, and additional pieces of torn and ink-stained cloth had recently been discovered there. What's more, ADA Haller told the court, "the police have learned that a Chinaman was seen within a few nights after the child disappeared on Delaware Avenue, coming southerly, between Scajaquada Creek bridge and Forest Avenue. This man was about the same size and stature as We."

Likely exasperated in full by this point, Justice Kenefick nonetheless wanted to perform a thorough review of the arguments and the affidavits prior to issuing his ruling, so at the close of the proceedings he announced that he would reserve his decision, to be arrived at and issued formally in the days to come.

Six days later, on Wednesday, August 6, it was declared that bail would not be granted, and that Charley We would in fact remain at the Erie County Jail until the grand jury assembled in another month's time. Period. Alongside his decision, the *Buffalo Evening News* reported, Justice Kenefick did not bother to include a written delineation of the logic which had brought him to his ruling. "I don't think the case is important enough to require an opinion," he briskly told the paper instead.

* * * * * *

The grand jury convened as scheduled at the county courthouse on Monday, September 8, taking up a number of "minor cases," the *Buffalo Evening News* reported, before finally delving into the grim and complicated specifics of the Marian Murphy murder.

On Friday, September 12, that body began reviewing the case against Charley We, the Chinese laundryman charged with the little girl's murder and held without bail ever since his arrest over two months previous. "As no information can be obtained from the officials connected with the case," the *Buffalo Evening Times* wrote, "it is impossible to learn from them what new evidence, if any, the People have against We." A slew of witnesses were called in, and these included Chief of Detectives Patrick Cusack, Detective John Devine of headquarters and a number of young children who resided in the vicinity of the Murphy home. "It is expected," the *Evening News* wrote later that afternoon, that "the grand jury will make its report on this and other cases next week."

The grand jury, however, wound up sitting in session throughout almost the entire month of September, hearing a number of criminal cases and waiting to issue reports until it had reviewed the particulars of each of the cases presented. The last bit of testimony was heard on Friday, September 26, and with that the grand jury was summarily dismissed and thanked for performing its civic duty. Written reports were expected right after the weekend, although a reporter from the *Buffalo Review* seems to have received an inside tip from a reliable source within the court system.

"Developments of yesterday presented what are, in all probability, unmistakable indications that the Grand Jury now sitting will indict no one to avenge the awful crime of the Marian Murphy murder," the *Review* revealed the following morning. "There is not the slightest reason to believe that a mandate of indictment will be issued against Charley We, the hapless Chinaman on whom the police, probably as a last resort, tried to fasten the crime by means of a miserably flimsy and far-fetched chain of circumstantial evidence."

The county courthouse was abuzz with activity on Monday, September 29, with the public and the press all gathered together outside County and City Hall, everyone assembled beneath the stately clock tower overlooking Franklin Street. The prisoner was brought over from the county jail, right behind the courthouse and across Delaware Avenue, ushered into the packed courtroom by Deputy Sheriff Allen F. Colby and entered into a row of other defendants with business before the grand jury.

Charley We was "togged in the height of Chinese fashion" when led in, the *Review* wrote, dressed "in black brocaded silk tunic, blue pantaloons and embroidered, rice-fibre slippers." The *Buffalo Express*, meanwhile, reported that "he looked quite sleek, with his pigtail done up neatly, his gray fedora hat, his black tunic, navy blue trousers and light green sandals with black brocade." Both papers agreed that he had thrived physically behind bars, with the *Express* describing him as "the same fat-faced full-bodied fellow he was when arrested" and the *Review* calling him "more rotund than ever."

We's eyes darted about, nervously checking out everything and everybody but he fastidiously avoided making direct eye contact. He "showed no sign of worry," the *Express* thought, "and now and then he half-grinned while he walked, some tip probably having reached him in the jail that the grand jury had not indicted him." The inmates were lined up, and the grand jury's spokesman began reading off the list of no-bills, naming the prisoners against whom no indictment had been returned and charges would not be pursued.

When We's name was called he stood, the *Review* wrote, although he "did not comprehend the proclamation which freed him from the guilt of the Murphy crime," and for "more than a minute he stood before the judge and did not move." Erie County Sheriff Francis Coppins then approached, whispering something into We's ear that caused the newly-exonerated to break into a grin that was ear-to-ear, if not downright Cheshire. Coppins, a 52-year-old locally-renowned artist, painter and decorator, had been appointed sheriff earlier in the year, and eagerly he clasped We's hand in what genuinely seemed to be earnest congratulations. As he did, the *Review* reported, "the Chink's face beamed and he laughed with hysterical joy."

Outside the courtroom attorney Hamilton Ward caught up with his client, and an informal reception was held right there in the cramped lobby. We, the *Express* noted, "found some difficulty in passing through the corridor to the elevator because of the number of men – all white men – who stopped him to shake hands and congratulate him." A horde of reporters crowded around, each of them asking We to comment on the wrongful accusations which had jammed him up all summer.

"Vely much glad," was all the laundryman would say, and he said it over and over again. "Me know nothing 'bout little gal. Policeman makes mistake."

When asked what he planned to do next, We indicated that he would be returning to his Hudson Street home, although the *Express* pointed out that the laundry had been sitting vacant since his arrest and by now "his business has gone to smash." Still, he told a *Review* reporter, perseverance would be his path forward, and he would reopen and rebuild his laundry with the discipline and the persistence his people were known to have carried with them from the Orient.

With that, the *Review* wrote, the laundryman stepped out of the courthouse and into the afternoon sun, "and We's going from the City Hall was a sort of triumphal exit."

TEN

An Ongoing Unraveling

No one knows, and no one ever will know, who carried Marian Murphy off to her cruel demise, then disposing of her remains in the water up at Forest Lawn Cemetery. Those answers would be forever lost to history, and the *Buffalo Review* was quick to admit that "it is not probable that the police can do much more work on the case," adding that "at this late date, with clues either dimmed or obliterated, the task would be a difficult one."

Police Superintendent Bull, when reached for comment at the district attorney's office, was predictably short and snippy in his statement. "We arrested Charley We for the crime," was his only remark, and it was clear that Bull and other police officials had been genuinely surprised by the grand jury's failure to indict.

Instead, the *Review* wrote, that body would most likely issue a "John Doe mandate," a charge against an unknown party lodged in the event of an eventual arrest. "It is significant," that paper wrote, "that for weeks after Charley We was arrested for the crime, and even after the evidence gathered against him had been turned over to the District Attorney's office, the police still worked on the Murphy case, and they did not confine their efforts entirely to finding more evidence against the accused Celestial. The police continued to pursue their efforts in the belief that others besides We participated in the murder. These others have never been run down."

The following day, September 30, the *Buffalo Evening News* ran a sobering editorial piece, acknowledging the release of Charley We and also chastising its competition for their rush to try a seemingly-innocent and perfectly nice man in the court of public opinion. From that editorial:

> The grand jury yesterday set free the Chinaman, Charley We, who has been in the Jail since the first of July under an unfounded accusation of murdering little Marian Murphy. He is said to be very happy. He ought to be. For there was so much prejudice against him and all Chinamen, caused by sensational reports and inflammatory appeals, that he was lucky in escaping mob violence. There was never a shred of evidence against him, as the NEWS pointed out at the time, and yet our American Boxers were so roused by announcements in certain papers that "Marian Murphy's Murder is Caught," and by dark hints of what the awful Chinaman had done, that the police authorities on the night of July 1 sent out word to all the Chinamen in Buffalo to keep in their houses, as there was danger of violence. The NEWS protested at the time against the stirring of race hatred, but

the condemnation of We on what the Commercial called a "priori evidence" went on to an extent never equaled in Buffalo.

Still, the article concluded: "Someone did kill that poor girl. Has the search for him been given up? Nothing has been done, so far as known, since all hands settled down content with having locked up poor We. It would be interesting to know what is doing, or likely to be done, now that a cool-headed grand jury has acquitted the Chinaman of even probable connection with the murder."

* * * * * *

To that end, actually, further investigation was taking place, however it was being done completely independent of the Buffalo Police Department. A firm of private detectives – "well and widely known here and in other cities," the *Buffalo Review* wrote – had come to town in the wake of Charley We's arrest, likely hired by the local Chinese contingent to help clear his name, although the firm's representatives would neither confirm nor deny this. Back in August the *Review* had interviewed one of these investigators, who had spoken on the condition of anonymity and made a few explosive claims regarding Marian Murphy's death and the policework done in response.

"We know things that will startle the City of Buffalo, if ever they are disclosed," bragged the dick, hastily adding that the persecution of Charley We was wholly unjust and completely uncalled for. "That arrest was the worst piece of rot ever perpetrated by the Police Department of this city."

It had since been learned, the man insisted, that Marian Murphy's death had been accidental, and that the considerable brutality done to the child's body had transpired after her demise, rather than as a precursor to it. That vicious assault, the *Review* wrote, "was done after death and was done for a purpose – and that purpose was to throw suspicion of the murder on some poor innocent like Charley We."

"That child was killed by accident," the detective stated conclusively. "That is the plain truth. She was subsequently assaulted in order that suspicion might be thrown on some other person."

This striking revelation, if true, turned things entirely on their head, and it completely obliterated the police department's established theory of motive. Whether or not the individual officers involved had truly believed in We's guilt, that detective stated, or whether they had knowingly participated in the railroading of innocent man for show, was, at this point, a matter of conjecture.

"But you have no idea, have you, that the police are not sincere in the charge which they have brought against the Chinaman?" the reporter challenged.

"Sincere?" the detective shot back, his voice dripping with sarcasm and incredulity. "Sincere? Well – I don't know whether they are sincere or not. I hate to think otherwise because I have always found Chief Cusack to be a shrewd and sagacious detective and I hate to think him not sincere because I know he is an honorable gentleman."

"Everybody thinks he is sincere," the *Review* man assured him. "If you talk to him about the case you will be impressed with his sincerity."

"Well," the investigator replied, "if he is sincere, I am surprised. I'll tell you one thing though, I'll bet you 10 to one his men aren't sincere. If Pat Cusack believes in the Chinaman's guilt, Pat Devine doesn't. Neither does that clever partner of his, Louis Henafelt. And there are plenty of others in the Department of Police who know for a dead sure thing that Charley We is as innocent of this charge as a babe unborn."

"Did the police learn everything it was possible to learn from the Murphy family and from the neighbors?" the reporter asked in follow-up.

"Well, I should say not," the detective replied. "If they had only found out where little Marian was accustomed to spend her time when she was out after 8 and 9 o'clock at night, and learn that only too often was the child on the street late at night, they would have run against an important clue."

"Does your clue lead you to suspect any particular person?"

"I hope you don't think I'm going to answer that," the unnamed investigator responded flatly. "I am telling you we know some startling things. I am sorry I told you that."

Other local professionals had been called on to participate during the investigation, and at least one of them would later state that he believed he had been able to ascertain the killer's identity. Dr. Nelson W. Wilson had done some work peripheral to the case, the *Buffalo Evening News* wrote, "retained by the defense to act in conjunction with Dr. John A. Miller in the analysis of the spots on the cloth found in Charley We's satchel, and which are said by Chemist Miller to resemble stains of washed-out blood."

Dr. Wilson, according to his 1915 obituary in that paper, was "formerly prominent in Buffalo newspaper circles and in later years one of the city's best known physicians." Born in Rutherford, New Jersey, he had worked as a print reporter in New York City – he'd been on staff at the *New York Star*, the *New York Morning Journal* and the *New York World* – before coming to Buffalo in the early 1890s to work for the *Evening News*. In addition to being an ambitious reporter, Wilson had served as secretary to the paper's publisher, Edward H. Butler, and eventually been made its city editor.

During his tenure at the *Evening News* Wilson had developed an interest in medicine, enrolling at the University of Buffalo and eventually claiming his degree, then exiting the newspaper business to pursue a career as a physician in that city. On staff at Buffalo General Hospital, his obituary stated, Wilson had been present at the Pan-Am Expo on the occasion of President McKinley's assassination and "was among the surgeons who first attended the nation's chief executive." He also had his own practice downtown near Niagara Square, and when called upon he had gladly lent his expertise in the examination of the physical evidence in the case against Charley We.

Dr. Wilson would eventually comment on the matter, although it would take him a full decade to do so, and even then the physician would decline to name any names. His remarks would come in the aftermath of another gruesome child murder, that of seven-year-old Joey Joseph in nearby Lackawanna, who in November 1912 was found raped, killed and stuffed down into an outhouse toilet behind a Ridge Road tavern. The newspapers, naturally, had started drawing some parallels between Joey's murder and Marian's, and it was at that time that Dr. Wilson felt compelled to speak up.

"There is a wide difference in the two cases," he told the *Buffalo Courier* on the morning of November 19, 1912. "Their only similarity lies in the fact that both were sexual crimes. The Josephs case was a high degree sadistic murder – a case where death or the mutilating of the victim was a necessity for the fulfillment of the sexual appetite of the murderer. It was not a killing as an accompaniment of rage or fear. The murder was as necessary a part of the assault as the attack itself."

"In the Marion Murphy case," he continued, "there was an assault of particularly sexual type. It was not necessarily the act of an invert. It was more the crime of a mental pervert and the killing which followed was the result of the suddenly awakened fear of an already diseased mind. Marion Murphy was strangled with the rope which bound her neck. She was not drowned."

Having thoroughly evaluated the Murphy case from this angle, Dr. Wilson declared the following: "I am fairly certain in my own mind, and I investigated the case from a sexuo-criminologic standpoint at the time, of the identity of the murderer, and he bore few if any of the stigmata of the true sexual invert."

Those remarks, inconclusive as they were, would be reviewed and assessed nearly a century later by a one-time police officer named Vance McLaughlin, who had gone on to become a law enforcement litigation consultant and was director of planning for the Savannah Police Department in Savannah, Georgia. In 2006 McLaughlin released *The Postcard Killer*, a book chronicling the Joey Joesph case and profiling his killer, an alcoholic and pedophilic engineer and drifter named J. Frank Hickey. McLaughlin dedicates a chapter of his book to the Murphy affair, and that chapter concludes with his interpretation of Dr. Wilson's suspicions:

"Based upon his education and training," McLaughlin felt, "Wilson would have convicted the same person the police initially focused on – her father, Cornelius Murphy."

McLaughlin is not alone in his belief that Cornelius had, after all, been the one responsible for his daughter's death. Richard Sullivan is a Hawaii-based author and photojournalist, a long-time (and award-winning) photographer for *Los Angeles Times Magazine* who has also issued a number of illustrated Hawaiian guidebooks. He also has direct ancestral ties to the Murphy case – his great-grandfather, Jim Sullivan, had been one of the detectives sent by headquarters to help with the tenth precinct's investigation, on hand for the arrest of Charley We as well as the subsequent search of his place.

Brilliantly, Richard Sullivan has used his lineage to produce *The First Ward*, a five-volume series of historical fiction books which follow his Irish ancestors through the earliest years of Buffalo's history. Upon their 1850 immigration to America the Sullivan family had settled in the notorious First Ward district, and the series follows brothers Jim and J.P. – a Buffalo police detective and a city alderman, respectively – as they navigate just about every notable event to hit the city through around 1930.

Volume three of this series, *Murderers, Scoundrels and Ragamuffins*, begins by exploring the Marian Murphy disappearance, spotlighting Detective Jim's involvement in the case and reviewing his long list of reasons for suspecting Cornelius's involvement. From that book:

"The police had devoted all their attention to the Chinaman only to have it determined he was not guilty after all. Jim from the beginning had deep suspicions regarding the dead girl's father due to Murphy's often bizarre and unexplained statements to detectives and his inscrutable behavior outside the house prior to notifying his wife of their child's body being found. He could account for neither his time nor his whereabouts coinciding with the hours of Marian's disappearance. An account of his activities published in the newspapers that appeared at first to exonerate him was found to have been fabricated. He made statements that implicated him in his interviews with reporters. He displayed aggression and unwarranted animosity toward the Gibbs family. He did not want his wife to be questioned without his being present. He maintained his wife in a state of stupor throughout."

And, from later in the book: "Jim made it his policy to stop by the Murphy family house on West Street whenever he was in the area to check on the children. He wanted to be sure that the Murphy daughters remained safe. He wanted Marian Murphy's father to know he was under Jim's suspicion and was being monitored closely. Murphy threatened to file a lawsuit. Jim was ordered by his superiors to stay away. Yet he still drove past the house given any opportunity regardless, stopping out front to make his message clear."

* * * * * *

The Murphys, actually, had been forced to relocate back in early August, pushed out of their small West Avenue home on account of their patriarch's inability to come up with the monthly rent payments.

Cornelius's employer, the *Catholic Union and Times*, had very generously granted him a leave of absence while he dealt with the extenuating circumstances of his daughter's death, but money had been tight to begin with and now, with that sad ordeal concluded, his creditors were just about through affording any grace. "At the time of little Marian's disappearance," the *Buffalo Review* noted, "Cornelius Murphy was in financial straits and was preparing to move from the West Avenue house because he could not pay his rent. The landlord, however, allowed the family to stay in the house during the terrible time and until Mrs. Murphy was well enough to be moved."

The space the family moved into was at 7 Wadsworth Street, several blocks away in the neighboring Allentown neighborhood, just across from Days Park and steps away from the foot of Allen Street. Better known as the Falcon Building, the small, nondescript, two-story brick structure (demolished in January 2008) provided the family temporary living quarters until something more suitable and long-term could be arranged.

By the following year, however, the Murphys were settled back into a more comfortable stead, and it was a place that was familiar to the family for a number of reasons – the house, a single-family dwelling located at 289 Pennsylvania Street, had been the Murphys' home prior to their moving into the West Avenue property, and it was literally just around the corner from that former address. It seems to have functioned as a boarding house, and its back yard backed right up into the side yard of the family's previous residence, the one with all the broken and traumatic memories now enshrining it.

There the family soldiered on, although much of what followed was perhaps inevitable. In the immediate aftermath of his daughter's disappearance, doctors had cautioned that Cornelius's psychological condition would continue to deteriorate, and that he ran the risk of becoming "permanently insane" later in life. And, sure enough, it took just seven years for another flare-up to spiral completely out of control, making the papers and landing Cornelius back in remand at Buffalo State Hospital.

From the May 1, 1909 edition of the *Buffalo Enquirer*:

Interest in the mysterious murder of little Marion Murphy, the 7-year-old girl who disappeared from her parents' home in West Avenue, in June, 1902, and whose body was subsequently found in a stream in Forest Lawn Cemetery, was revived in police circles today, when her father, Cornelius V. Murphy, was arrested after a fierce struggle on a charge of insanity. Murphy, under the watchful eye of Turnkey Conley, is in a straightjacket in the cellroom of the Pearl Street Police Station. He will be examined by Police Surgeon Bowerman and committed to an asylum.

Murphy is about 45 years old, and lives with his family at No. 289 Pennsylvania Street. He is a solicitor for a local newspaper.

This morning, shortly before 9 o'clock he went into the business office of the newspaper company and talked and acted so irrationally that the girls employed there grew afraid of him. They called up the West Seneca Street Police Station on a telephone and asked for a policeman to take the man away. Detective Jack Murray went to the place.

When Murray attempted to persuade Murphy to leave the office, the former leaped to his feet, aimed a vicious blow at the officer, and then clinched with him. The men battled for ten minutes, Murray, who is a powerful man, finally overcoming Murphy.

The detective had to hold Murphy down on the pavement until the patrol wagon from No. 1 Police Station arrived. The frenzied man was handcuffed and carried into the wagon. On the way to the Pearl Street Station, Murphy got on to his feet and put up a fierce fight for his freedom. It took the efforts of Detective Murray, Patrolmen Hooley, Shields and Michael Murphy and Wagon Driver Stanton to subdue him.

The disappearance of little Marion Murphy, in 1902, was one of the biggest sensations in the country and one of the most mysterious cases that ever baffled the local Police Department. She was gone for three weeks, when her body was discovered in a little stream that flows through Forest Lawn Cemetery. The child had been outraged before she was killed and the body was horribly mutilated when it was found.

Suspicion pointed to no person in particular, but several were taken into custody by the police, one being a Chinese laundryman. He was subsequently released and ever since that time the child's death has been veiled in the mystery that first surrounded it.

Cornelius Murphy, the girl's father, has been in an asylum for the insane on several occasions.

The police learned later that Murphy, when he left home early today, told his wife that he was going down to the Catholic Union and Times office to kill W.A. King, business manager of the company. She had telephoned to the Niagara Street Police Station for the police to be on the lookout for her husband.

With her husband now institutionalized for the fourth time, Mary gathered up her three remaining children and quit Buffalo, fleeing east to Syracuse to live with Cornelius's sister and her husband, Art Spaulding. This placed fifteen-year-old Angela, the eldest Murphy child, on a fast track to young adulthood, prompting her to develop a deep, almost maternal concern for her younger brothers Leo and John, whom she looked after and cared for as if they were her own. Having weathered two devastating losses – first the death of her beloved younger sister and, now, a sudden relocation and separation from her father – the girl also became acutely devoted to her mother, tending to her obsessively and forgoing marriage until after Mary had passed away.

Cornelius Murphy died in his Pennsylvania Street home on May 13, 1918. His hometown newspaper, the *Fulton Patriot*, took note of his passing, mentioning that he had begun his career at that publication before moving to Buffalo to work for the *Catholic Union and Times*. He was fifty-four years old at the time of his death, and his remains were transported back to Fulton for internment at St. Mary's Cemetery.

Epilogue

Tuesday, October 28 was a chilly fall morning, and the children of the Lakeview neighborhood were scurrying about in preparation for All Hallow's Eve, that spooky and mischievous night of tricks and treats and costumed youngsters going door to door.

A month had passed since Charley We had been freed from the Erie County Jail, and, true to his word, the papers found him that day at 285 Hudson Street, busily readying his establishment to re-open that very afternoon. "In the face of neighborhood antagonism," the *Buffalo Courier* wrote, "in the face of ruined business, We went about re-establishing himself with an air of cheerfulness. Many people stopped and, looking in, wondered at the courage of the Oriental. To all these We returned with a smile and an explanation that his arrest was all a mistake; that he intended to do business 'allee samee as ever,' and that he hoped to regain his lost patronage."

A reporter from the *Buffalo Evening News* stopped by, and We spoke with him briefly about the challenges of rebuilding in the aftermath of his devastating arrest and imprisonment. That whole ordeal, We estimated, from the three months of lost business to the considerable damage done to his place by police and others, as well as all the legal fees, had cost him roughly $1,000. It was his intent, We stated, to pursue a claim against the city for these damages.

"When the police took me to jail I asked them to watch my place," he explained. "They did not do it and everything was destroyed. I haven't a cent to my name now. I think the city ought to pay me for what I have lost, at least ought to give me enough to start in business again." (It is interesting to note that, in the aftermath of Charley We's exoneration, the *Evening News* was quick to change its approach, suddenly extending him the courtesy of neatly Americanized verbiage.)

Inside, the *Courier* wrote, We was "busy refurnishing the laundry establishment," while just outside the house pedestrians strolled past, some of them wondering aloud how the determined laundryman would fare moving forward. "It's dangerous for him to reopen that place," one of them was heard to say. "Somebody will blow it up at night. I feel sorry for that Chinaman, but he's got a lot of courage."

Throughout the day numerous children "romped in front of the place," that paper added, although nervous mothers periodically could be heard calling for their young ones to come away from there. One of these kids, pausing to speak with the *Courier* reporter, giddily indicated the We house and told of earlier exchanges with its exotic proprietor.

"He used to give us candy," the kid exclaimed, pointing through a window and gesturing at the fastidious laborer inside.

Epilogue

Just then a boy came rushing up from out of nowhere, sneaking up on all the kids gathered there and taking the lot of them by surprise.

"Boo!" he shouted, popping up abruptly amidst his startled companions.

Little girls shrieked and scattered in every direction.

Acknowledgments

This book would not have been possible without a bit of help.

The majority of the research was performed in the Grosvenor Room at the Buffalo and Erie County Public Library, with assistance from its very helpful and knowledgeable staff. Additional research was done at fulton-history.com, an invaluable online resource of archived early newsprint.

Cynthia Van Ness, director of library and archives at the Buffalo History Museum, very kindly provided me with a digital copy of the 1902 Buffalo City Directory. I also had access to the vast records of ancestry.com, thanks to a subscription given to me by my mother, Joan M. Elevich. It was largely thanks to her encouragement that I pursued the writing of nonfiction, and I am very grateful for her ongoing support.

John Edens, a director at the Forest Lawn Heritage Foundation, very graciously provided me with a plethora of information relating to that cemetery's history. The staff at Holy Cross Cemetery were similarly helpful in accessing Marian Murphy's burial records.

Lastly, the creation of this book was greatly enhanced by my correspondence with Jeanne Shanahan, the granddaughter of Marian's older sister Jane. Jeanne grew up very close to her grandmother, whom she said spoke of her sister often and was affected profoundly by her disappearance. This book is very much a product of Jeanne's willingness to share with me her family's history and her grandmother's recollections.

Sources

PROLOGUE

- Polk's Buffalo City Directory, 1902.
- "Marion Murphy's Body Found In Forest Lawn Lake," Buffalo Courier, June 28, 1902.
- "Marion Murphy's Body Found In Forest Lawn Cemetery Bound Hand And Foot," Buffalo Evening News, June 28, 1902.
- "Marian Murphy Brutally Murdered," Buffalo Evening Times, June 28, 1902.
- "Weaving The Woof In Murder Mystery," Buffalo Courier, June 29, 1902.
- "Judge Murphy Decides To Issue Warrant For We," Buffalo Evening News, July 7, 1902.
- "A Short History of Forest Lawn Cemetery," buffaloah.com (website). Accessed online at https://buffaloah.com/a/forestL/fl.html

ONE – A West Side Story

- Polk's Buffalo City Directory, 1902.
- "Troubles Of 'Con' Murphy," Buffalo Evening News, June 10, 1899.
- "Murphy In The Asylum," Buffalo Express, July 9, 1899.
- "Detectives Are Searching For Missing Child," Buffalo Evening Times, June 18, 1902.

- "Deep Mystery In The Child's Disappearance," Buffalo Courier, June 19, 1902.
- "School Teacher Saw Missing Girl At The Front," Buffalo Evening News, June 19, 1902.
- "Women In Black Seen Leading A Crying Child," Buffalo Evening Times, June 19, 1902.
- "Strange Disappearance Of Marian Murphy," Buffalo Review, June 19, 1902.
- "Kidnaped By Mistake By Notorious 'Lon' Whiteman May Be Marian Murphy's Fate," Buffalo Courier, June 20, 1902.
- "Dragging Canal For Missing Girl," Buffalo Evening News, June 20, 1902.
- "Lon Whiteman Not A Kidnaper," Buffalo Evening Times, June 20, 1902.
- "Child Was Kidnaped By Mistake," Buffalo Review, June 20, 1902.
- "Hundreds Will Throng Canal Bank Looking For Marian Murphy," Buffalo Evening Times, June 22, 1902.
- "Marion Murphy's Body Found In Forest Lawn Lake," Buffalo Courier, June 28, 1902.
- "Marian Murphy Brutally Murdered," Buffalo Evening Times, June 28, 1902.
- "Weaving The Woof In Murder Mystery," Buffalo Courier, June 29, 1902.
- "Murphy Murder Mystery Deepens," Buffalo Evening Times, June 29, 1902.
- "Assaulted, Then Strangled To Death," Buffalo Courier, June 30, 1902.

Sources

- "We's Comrade Has Skipped Out," Buffalo Evening Times, July 6, 1902.
- "Judge Murphy Decides To Issue Warrant For We," Buffalo Evening News, July 7, 1902.
- "Charlie We Held For The Murder," Buffalo Evening Times, July 7, 1902.
- "We, The Chinaman, Held For First Degree Murder By Justice Murphy," Buffalo Courier, July 8, 1902.
- "'Not Guilty,' The Plea Of Charlie We," Buffalo Evening News, July 8, 1902.
- "Sensational Developments Promised Shortly In The Marian Murphy Murder," Buffalo Review, August 11, 1902.
- McLaughlin, Vance, The Postcard Killer. New York: Thunder's Mouth Press, 2006.
- "Torn-Down Tuesday: The Fargo Mansion, home of a Wells Fargo founder," Buffalo Evening News, July 11, 2017.
- Hix, Lisa, "Masher Menace: When American Women First Confronted Their Sexual Harassers," Collectors Weekly (website), December 14, 2017. Accessed online at https://www.collectorsweekly.com/articles/when-american-women-first-confronted-their-sexual-harassers/
- "Buffalo, NY Police Precincts," Buffalo Police Then and Now (website). Accessed online at http://www.bpdthenandnow.com/precinctbuildings.html
- "Fargo Mansion – Then & Now," Western New York Heritage (website). Accessed online at https://www.wnyheritage.org/content/fargo_mansion_-_then_now/index.html

- "A Lost Buffalo Landmark: The Fargo Mansion," Buffalo Rising (website). Accessed online at https://www.buffalorising.com/2020/09/a-lost-buffalo-landmark-the-fargo-mansion/
- "Population of the 100 Largest Cities and Other Urban Places In The United States: 1790 to 1990," United States Census Bureau (website). Accessed online at https://www.census.gov/library/working-papers/1998/demo/POP-twps0027.html

TWO – A Neighborhood Frenzy

- Polk's Buffalo City Directory, 1902.
- "Six-Year-Old Child Missing," Buffalo Courier, June 18, 1902.
- "Detectives Are Searching For Missing Child," Buffalo Evening Times, June 18, 1902.
- "Deep Mystery In The Child's Disappearance," Buffalo Courier, June 19, 1902.
- "School Teacher Saw Missing Girl At The Front," Buffalo Evening News, June 19, 1902.
- "Women In Black Seen Leading A Crying Child," Buffalo Evening Times, June 19, 1902.
- "Strange Disappearance Of Marian Murphy," Buffalo Review, June 19, 1902.
- "Kidnaped By Mistake By Notorious 'Lon' Whiteman May Be Marian Murphy's Fate," Buffalo Courier, June 20, 1902.
- "Dragging Canal For Missing Girl," Buffalo Evening News, June 20, 1902.
- "Following Up Many Clues To Find Missing Girl," Buffalo Evening News, June 20, 1902.

Sources

- "Lon Whiteman Not A Kidnaper," Buffalo Evening Times, June 20, 1902.

- "Child Was Kidnaped By Mistake," Buffalo Review, June 20, 1902.

- "Gibbs Departure Very Mysterious," Buffalo Evening Times, June 21, 1902.

- "Hundreds Will Throng Canal Bank Looking For Marian Murphy," Buffalo Evening Times, June 22, 1902.

- "Marion Murphy's Body Found In Forest Lawn Lake," Buffalo Courier, June 28, 1902.

- "Postcard From Buffalo: Terrace Park, 1902, or What was there before the Skyway," Greater Buffalo (website), September 16, 2019. Accessed online at https://greaterbuffalo.blogs.com/gbb/2019/09/postcard-from-buffalo-terrace-park-1902.html

- Nelson, Paul, "'As a liar he is a phenomenon': Alonzo J. Whiteman's journey from Duluth businessman to career criminal," MinnPost (website), January 31, 2022. Accessed online at https://www.minnpost.com/mnopedia/2022/01/as-a-liar-he-is-a-phenomenon-alonzo-j-whitemans-journey-from-duluth-businessman-to-career-criminal/

- "The Front (Front Park)," Olmsted In Buffalo (website). Accessed online at https://www.olmstedinbuffalo.com/the-front-front-park/?fbclid=IwAR2iaF70zRjofBE1bIKVK-GDsiKLDSMMDBXKwB9q5dudiZjK5REgtQPQInQk

THREE – Dead Ends

- Polk's Buffalo City Directory, 1902.
- "Dragging Canal For Missing Girl," Buffalo Evening News, June 20, 1902.
- "Lon Whiteman Not A Kidnaper," Buffalo Evening Times, June 20, 1902.
- "Child Was Kidnaped By Mistake," Buffalo Review, June 20, 1902.
- "Reward Of $1,000 For Marian Murphy Offered By Friends," Buffalo Courier, June 21, 1902.
- "Reward Offered For The Return Of Missing Girl," Buffalo Evening News, June 21, 1901.
- "Gibbs Departure Very Mysterious," Buffalo Evening Times, June 21, 1902.
- "Not One Clue To Tell Mother Of Missing Child," Buffalo Courier, June 22, 1902.
- "Hundreds Will Throng Canal Bank Looking For Marian Murphy," Buffalo Evening Times, June 22, 1902.
- "Louis Tolinski Found In The Almshouse," Buffalo Evening News, June 23, 1902.
- "Police Give Up Hope Of Finding Missing Girl," Buffalo Evening Times, June 23, 1902.
- "Pray For Return Of Marian Murphy," Buffalo Evening Times, June 23, 1902.
- "Eight Days Since Child Disappeared," Buffalo Evening News, June 24, 1902.
- "Police Admit All Work Is Through," Buffalo Review, June 27, 1902.

- "Weaving The Woof In Murder Mystery," Buffalo Courier, June 29, 1902.
- "Evidence Is Weak Against Chinamen," Buffalo Evening News, July 2, 1902.
- "Gathering Evidence," Buffalo Evening Times, July 2, 1902.
- "Saw Chinaman Near Where Girl's Body Was Found," Buffalo Evening News, July 3, 1902.
- "Not Blood Stains On Charlie We's Wall," Buffalo Evening News, July 7, 1902.
- "Charlie We Held For The Murder," Buffalo Evening Times, July 7, 1902.
- "Valerian," Mount Sinai (website). Accessed online at https://www.mountsinai.org/health-library/herb/valerian

FOUR – "Her Little Soul's In Heaven"

- Polk's Buffalo City Directory, 1902.
- "Marion Murphy's Body Found In Forest Lawn Lake," Buffalo Courier, June 28, 1902.
- "Marion Murphy's Body Found In Forest Lawn Cemetery Bound Hand And Foot," Buffalo Evening News, June 28, 1902.
- "Marian Murphy Brutally Murdered," Buffalo Evening Times, June 28, 1902.
- "Mary Murphy's Body Found," Buffalo Express, June 28, 1902.
- "George Troup Missed From His Old Post," Buffalo Evening News, July 6, 1913.
- "Judge Murphy Decides To Issue Warrant For We," Buffalo Evening News, July 7, 1902.

- "Not Blood Stains On Charlie We's Wall," Buffalo Evening News, July 7, 1902.
- "Charlie We Held For The Murder," Buffalo Evening Times, July 7, 1902.
- "Buffalo, NY Police Precincts," Buffalo Police Then and Now (website). Accessed online at http://www.bpdthenandnow.com/precinctbuildings.html
- "George Earl Danser," WikiTree (website). Accessed online at https://www.wikitree.com/wiki/Danser-34
- "A Short History of Forest Lawn Cemetery," buffaloah.com (website). Accessed online at https://buffaloah.com/a/forestL/fl.html

FIVE – Formalities

- Polk's Buffalo City Directory, 1902.
- "Council May Give Reward Of $1,000," Buffalo Courier, June 24, 1902.
- "Eight Days Since Child Disappeared," Buffalo Evening News, June 24, 1902.
- "Times Reporters On Police Boat Search For Little Marian," Buffalo Evening Times, June 25, 1902.
- "Marion Murphy's Body Found In Forest Lawn Lake," Buffalo Courier, June 28, 1902.
- "Marion Murphy's Body Found In Forest Lawn Cemetery Bound Hand And Foot," Buffalo Evening News, June 28, 1902.
- "Marian Murphy Brutally Murdered," Buffalo Evening Times, June 28, 1902.

Sources

- "Mary Murphy's Body Found," Buffalo Express, June 28, 1902.
- "Weaving The Woof In Murder Mystery," Buffalo Courier, June 29, 1902.
- "Murphy Murder Mystery Deepens," Buffalo Evening Times, June 29, 1902.
- "Assaulted, Then Strangled To Death," Buffalo Courier, June 30, 1902.
- "Marian Murphy Choked To Death," Buffalo Evening News, June 30, 1902.
- "Negro Arrested In Murphy Case," Buffalo Evening News, June 30, 1902.
- "Autopsy's Revelations," Buffalo Express, June 30, 1902.
- "Marian's Mother And The Murphys' Servant Closely Questioned," Buffalo Evening News, July 1, 1902.
- "Police Arrest Celestials On Suspicion Murphy Murder," Buffalo Evening Times, July 1, 1902.
- "Rewards Are Only $1,000," Buffalo Express, July 1, 1902.
- "$2,000 Is Offered For Capture Of Murderers," Buffalo Review, July 1, 1902.
- "Gathering Evidence," Buffalo Evening Times, July 2, 1902.
- "Judge Murphy Decides To Issue Warrant For We," Buffalo Evening News, July 7, 1902.
- "Not Blood Stains On Charlie We's Wall," Buffalo Evening News, July 7, 1902.
- "Charlie We Held For The Murder," Buffalo Evening Times, July 7, 1902.
- "Remember The Feet; Forget The Faces," Buffalo Courier, July 13, 1902.

- "Chinaman We To Be Given A Court Hearing," Buffalo Evening Times, July 16, 1902.
- "Holy Cross Cemetery," Catholic Cemeteries Dioceses of Buffalo (website). Accessed online at https://www.buffalocatholiccemeteries.org/holy-cross-cemetery

SIX – Zeroing In

- Polk's Buffalo City Directory, 1902.
- "Marian's Mother And The Murphys' Servant Closely Questioned," Buffalo Evening News, July 1, 1902.
- "Police Arrest Celestials On Suspicion Murphy Murder," Buffalo Evening Times, July 1, 1902.
- "Chinese Laundry Slaughter Pen Revealed By Milkman's Story," Buffalo Courier, July 2, 1902.
- "Evidence Is Weak Against Chinaman," Buffalo Evening News, July 2, 1902.
- "Gathering Evidence," Buffalo Evening Times, July 2, 1902.
- "Marian Murphy's Murderer Taken," Buffalo Review, July 2, 1902.
- "A Chinaman Had Basket On Car," Buffalo Courier, July 5, 1902.
- "Chinaman Skips," Buffalo Evening Times, July 5, 1902.
- "Arraigned! Chinaman We Enters A Plea Of Not Guilty," Buffalo Evening Times, July 8, 1902.
- "Chinaman Must Spend The Summer In Jail," Buffalo Evening News, July 10, 1902.

- "Trouble Impending In Chinese Colony," Buffalo Review, July 22, 1902.
- "Real American Celestial Is King Of Buffalo's Chinatown," Buffalo Courier, October 19, 1902.
- Miller, Greg, "1885 Map Reveals Vice in San Francisco's Chinatown and Racism at City Hall," Wired (website), September 30, 2013. Accessed online at https://www.wired.com/2013/09/1885-map-san-francisco-chinatow/
- "Buffalo Chinese History," Consider the Source New York (website). Accessed online at https://considerthesourceny.org/using-primary-sources/legacies/chinese-legacies/buffalo-chinese-legacy/buffalo-chinese-history
- Cichon, Steve "Torn-Down Tuesday: In 1940s, 'Chinese of Buffalo' gather at 507 Michigan," Buffalo Stories (website). Accessed online at http://blog.buffalostories.com/torn-down-tuesday-in-1940s-chinese-of-buffalo-gather-at-507-michigan/?fbclid=IwAR1gjBSM2oOndgVmAssmkiZytrb2XBhpJo9Dp_gShyrRkjk3l5HkdGn-Ex8

SEVEN – Due Diligence

- Polk's Buffalo City Directory, 1902.
- "Chinese Laundry Slaughter Pen Revealed By Milkman's Story," Buffalo Courier, July 2, 1902.
- "Evidence Is Weak Against Chinaman," Buffalo Evening News, July 2, 1902.
- "Gathering Evidence," Buffalo Evening Times, July 2, 1902.

- "Marian Murphy's Murderer Taken," Buffalo Review, July 2, 1902.
- "Marian Murphy Was Killed In The Block In Which Is Located The Chinese Laundry," Buffalo Courier, July 3, 1902.
- "Saw Chinaman Near Where Girl's Body Was Found," Buffalo Evening News, July 3, 1902.
- "'I'd Arrest The Mayor On The Evidence I Had," Buffalo Evening Times, July 3, 1902.
- "Police All Insist Case Is Stronger Against Chinaman," Buffalo Courier, July 4, 1902.
- "Hard To Hold We," Buffalo Express, July 4, 1902.
- "A Chinaman Had Basket On Car," Buffalo Courier, July 5, 1902.
- "Chinaman May Be Released On Monday," Buffalo Evening News, July 5, 1902.
- "Chinaman Skips," Buffalo Evening Times, July 5, 1902.
- "Police Get Another Clue," Buffalo Express, July 5, 1902.
- "After The Long Wait An Inquest Will Be Held In Marian Murphy Case," Buffalo Courier, July 6, 1902.
- "We's Comrade Has Skipped Out," Buffalo Evening Times, July 6, 1902.
- "This Clue Vague," Buffalo Express, July 6, 1902.
- "Arraigned! Chinaman We Enters A Plea Of Not Guilty," Buffalo Evening Times, July 8, 1902.
- "Real American Celestial Is King Of Buffalo's Chinatown," Buffalo Courier, October 19, 1902.
- Lane, Louis B., History of the Bench and Bar of Erie County New York. Buffalo: The Genealogical Publishing Company, 1909.

- "Hamilton Ward, Distinguished Lawyer, Dies," Buffalo Courier-Express, October 9, 1932.
- "Sympathy Is Widespread At Death of Hamilton Ward," Buffalo Evening News, October 10, 1932.
- "Buffalo Chinese History," Consider the Source New York (website). Accessed online at https://considerthesourceny. org/using-primary-sources/legacies/chinese-legacies/buffalo-chinese-legacy/buffalo-chinese-history
- Cichon, Steve "Torn-Down Tuesday: In 1940s, 'Chinese of Buffalo' gather at 507 Michigan," Buffalo Stories (website). Accessed online at http://blog.buffalostories.com/torn-down-tuesday-in-1940s-chinese-of-buffalo-gather-at-507-michigan/?fbclid=IwAR1gjBSM2oOndgVmAssmkiZytrb2XBhpJo9Dp_gShyrRkjk3l5HkdGn-Ex8

EIGHT – Legal Maneuvering

- Polk's Buffalo City Directory, 1902.
- "Chinaman May Be Released On Monday," Buffalo Evening News, July 5, 1902.
- "Judge Murphy Decides To Issue Warrant For We," Buffalo Evening News, July 7, 1902.
- "Charlie We Held For The Murder," Buffalo Evening Times, July 7, 1902.
- "We, The Chinaman, Held For First Degree Murder By Justice Murphy," Buffalo Courier, July 8, 1902.
- "'Not Guilty,' The Plea Of Charlie We," Buffalo Evening News, July 8, 1902.

- "Arraigned! Chinaman We Enters A Plea Of Not Guilty," Buffalo Evening Times, July 8, 1902.
- "Chinese Suspect Held," Buffalo Express, July 8, 1902.
- "We Re-Arraigned And Held For The Grand Jury," Buffalo Evening News, July 9, 1902.
- "We Pleads Not Guilty; Asks Trial," Buffalo Evening Times, July 9, 1902.
- "We Was Arraigned," Buffalo Review, July 9, 1902.
- "Want To Erect A Memorial Tablet On Marian's Grave," Buffalo Evening Times, July 10, 1902.
- "Failed To Liberate We," Buffalo Express, July 10, 1902.
- "Remember The Feet; Forget The Faces," Buffalo Courier, July 13, 1902.
- "Charlie We Is Happier In Jail," Buffalo Evening News, July 14, 1902.

NINE – A Chinaman's Chance

- Polk's Buffalo City Directory, 1902.
- "Marian Murphy's Murderer Taken," Buffalo Review, July 2, 1902.
- "Blotches Of Human Blood Are Red Spots On Cloth Found In Chinese Laundry," Buffalo Courier, July 9, 1902.
- "No Blood Found On Rags From We's Laundry," Buffalo Evening News, July 9, 1902.
- "A Fruitless Search For Marian's Dress," Buffalo Evening News, July 11, 1902.

- "Dragging Lake To Find Marian Murphy's Dress," Buffalo Evening News, July 11, 1902.
- "Marian's Clothes Not In The Sewer," Buffalo Evening Times, July 11, 1902.
- "Not Much Evidence," Buffalo Review, July 11, 1902.
- "Do The Lines Of Charley We's Hands Show Him To Be A Brutal, Crafty Murderer," Buffalo Evening Times, July 13, 1902.
- "Charlie We Is Happier In Jail," Buffalo Evening News, July 14, 1902.
- "We To Have Hearing Today," Buffalo Courier, July 16, 1902.
- "Habeas Corpus In The Case Of The Chinaman," Buffalo Evening News, July 16, 1902.
- "We's Lawyer Gets Writ Of Habeas Corpus," Buffalo Evening News, July 16, 1902.
- "Chinaman We To Be Given A Court Hearing," Buffalo Evening Times, July 16, 1902.
- "Charlie We May Get His Freedom Today," Buffalo Courier, July 17, 1902.
- "Charlie We Produced By Sheriff In Court," Buffalo Evening News, July 17, 1902.
- "Extra! Extra! We Held For Grand Jury," Buffalo Evening Times, July 17, 1902.
- "Judge Kenefick Dismisses Writ In We's Case," Buffalo Evening News, July 17, 1902.
- "Back To Jail Sentence For We," Buffalo Courier, July 18, 1902.
- "Today Is The Birthday Of Little Marian Murphy," Buffalo Evening Times, July 18, 1902.
- "Police Have More Evidence On Chink," Buffalo Evening Times, July 31, 1902.

- "No Bail For Charlie We," Buffalo Evening News, August 6, 1902.
- "We's Case Before Grand Jury Today," Buffalo Evening Times, September 12, 1902.
- "Murphy Murder Case Before Grand Jury," Buffalo Evening News, September 13, 1902.
- "Charley We Goes Free," Buffalo Express, September 30, 1902.
- "Chinaman We Not Indicted," Buffalo Review, September 30, 1902.
- "Daniel J Kenefick – Buffalo War Council," Wikipedia Commons (website). Accessed online at https://commons.wikimedia.org/wiki/File:Daniel_J_Kenefick_-_Buffalo_War_Council.jpg
- "Daniel Joseph Kenefick (1863)," WikiTree (website). Accessed online at https://www.wikitree.com/wiki/Kenefick-23
- "History – Richmond Avenue Methodist Episcopal Church," buffaloah.com (website). Accessed Online at https://buffaloah.com/a/wferry/525/hist.html

TEN – An Ongoing Unraveling

- Polk's Buffalo City Directory, 1902 through 1909.
- "A Fruitless Search For Marian's Dress," Buffalo Evening News, July 11, 1902.
- "No Indictment For Charley We," Buffalo Review, September 27, 1902.
- "The Chinaman Is Free – What Next?" Buffalo Evening News, September 30, 1902.

Sources

- "Chinaman We Not Indicted," Buffalo Review, September 30, 1902.
- "Sensational Developments Promised Shortly In The Marian Murphy Murder," Buffalo Review, August 11, 1902.
- "Disappearance Of Marion Murphy Is Recalled," Buffalo Enquirer, May 1, 1909.
- "Dr. Wilson Denies Cases Are Similar," Buffalo Courier, November 19, 1912.
- "Dr. N. W. Wilson Dies While At Gotham Play," Buffalo Evening News, August 11, 1915.
- "Buffalo Physician Dies In A Theatre," New York Times, August 31, 1915.
- "Obituary Mention" (Cornelius Murphy)," Fulton Patriot, May 15, 1918.
- McLaughlin, Vance, The Postcard Killer. New York: Thunder's Mouth Press, 2006.
- Sullivan, Richard, The First Ward III: Murderers, Scoundrels and Ragamuffins. Montgomery Ewing Publishers, 2018.
- "Falcon Building," Preservation-Ready Site Buffalo (website). Accessed online at https://www.preservationready.org/Buildings/7WadsworthStreet
- Nussbaumer, Newell, "The Falcon Gets The Kiss Of Death," Buffalo Rising (website). Accessed online at https://www.buffalorising.com/2008/01/the-falcon-gets-the-kiss-of-death/

EPILOGUE

- "We Thinks City Owes Him Damages," Buffalo Evening News, October 28, 1902.
- "Charlie We Picks Up His Courage And Reopens His Laundry," Buffalo Courier, October 29, 1902.